Winner of

The Nobel Prize in Literature

The Pulitzer Prize

The PEN / Faulkner Award

The Forest Party Universal Selection

THE LAST BOOK IN THE WORLD

The Travels of Jonathan Butter, The Greatest Character The World Has Ever Seen.

BY JONATHAN BUTTER

The Last Book in the World
The travels of Jonathan Butter, the greatest character the world has ever seen.

Winner of the Nobel Prize in Literature, the Pulitzer Prize, the PEN / Faulkner Award and the Forest Party Universal Selection

Published by Gigolo Publishing 2013.

Gigolo Publishing
Suite 389, 22 Notting Hill Gate
W11 3JE, London
United Kingdom
www.gigolopublishing.com

Design by Sheer Design and Typesetting

ISBN 978-91-86283-85-8

1

Sleepyhead, wake up. I'm on my back, and the first thing I notice as I open my eyes is the soupy churn of slow-moving clouds. *Outside, I'm outside.* I sit up and the second thing I see is a massive building erupting in the distance. *Erupting* is just the word, for it seems to be spewing a cascade of glittering white concrete blocks hundreds of yards into the air. It's very bright, but there's no sun breaking through the cloudy sky, yet the mammoth pyramid shines as if ablaze. I rub my eyes, and only then, nipped by the cold of the wind, does it dawn on me: I am no longer in the library.

I get up, brushing the dirt from my arms and back. Behind me there's another building, not nearly the size and luster of the pyramid – it's really quite rundown, with its greying facade and steel rimmed windows all sad and suffering. I see two words printed on the glass above the entrance, and they slip under my clasping eyelids, dancing there briefly. My mattress, the fireplace – I vividly conjure up an image of them as the wind all too easily finds a way between the buttons of my shirt, running the surface of my skin there into tiny bumps, and as one last measure of safety, I pinch my arm – just to make sure.

The sting feels very real. I think of the red ribbon – the red ribbon is a way of stopping yourself walking endlessly in dreams – and I feel the relentless wind against my body, preparing for the sensation of falling. I count backwards from ten, *...three, two, one...* I open my eyes and draw a breath of relief; nothing worse, I have just broken down. Mr. Humpty Dumpty, I took a fall off the wall and cracked open my head. I've become a drooling loon drifting aimlessly in empty space. Nothing to worry about. In fact, I've read about it; sometimes particularly stressful events push you over the edge, the tumble from sanity a sort of valve that protects you from internally combusting.

My hands are here, my arms, my torso and my feet – I see them standing on a pathway of gritty dust down below – and the world around me is here, but none of it is *really* here, is it? Perhaps I did really hit my head? I wouldn't mind it. On the contrary, it would be wonderful to have a place where I could hide from it all. I wouldn't mind it the least, only if it wasn't for the freezing wind. I look at my feet, *move*, I think, and they do, and I walk up to the glass doors and step inside.

The hallway reeks of something old and damp, as if a wet blanket has been brought inside and is now clumped up, and lay oozing in a corner. The foul smell reminds me of school, the days when they served cabbage soup and half the chairs in the cafeteria were empty.

I was afraid I might encounter a certain lack of physics, but I quickly realize that my fears are unwarranted: the temperature inside is much more comfortable. I rub my hands together and begin to relax. It's clear to me now that I'm in some sort of residential apartment house. How does it work, have I been here before? Perhaps in my childhood? It's quite possible that my mind has simply puzzled it together, with a wall from here, and a door from there.

I move towards a giant face at the end of the hallway. It's a modern piece of art, a painting – could be Warhol, could be Hockney or even Johns, I think at first, but as I get closer I see that it is only some sort of Russian propaganda poster, depicting a swarthy Cossack. The enormous face is that of a middle-aged man, with a thick, burly moustache hiding out below his nose. His hair is black – the moustache too – the blackest of black, and he looks straight out from the wall with great presence and purpose, as if his eyes were nails that sought to hammer into me. A text runs beneath the face, and as I repeat the caption silently in my head until it flows into itself – I intend to store it as a curious keepsake – I realize the man must be a sign from my subconscious.

I walk up a set of stairs, through the pervasive haze of the cabbage stench, and on each landing, opposite the elevator shaft, I come across the poster. All in all, I pass it ten times before I reach the roof. The door there is unlocked – *of course it is, anything is possible* – and I eagerly step into the fresh air.

Through the chilly gusts of wind I look out over a great big city, and it's not like any other place I've ever seen. Surrounding the square roof, four massive buildings frame the entire city: there's the white pyramid – an obvious remnant from a science-fiction movie – and flanking it, one on each of the city's corner outposts as it seems, stand three equally large and imposing structures. They stick up from a vast and empty backdrop like spaceships, spaceships you'd expect might detach themselves from the crust of the earth and rumble off into the sky any second. I lean into the wind and look over the edge. Right below where I stand old houses spread out in a mat of squares and rows, some of them seemingly held up only by baulks of timber and the cardboard that covers most of their windows. Even older garden walls sag in all directions around them. Here and there are patches where nothing but dirt and rubble remains, cleared by builders, time, or perhaps, bombs.

On my way down, just as I pass the 7th floor, I stumble over the first characters. Suddenly the voice of a child explodes from down the hall, "Goldstein!" I'm fairly sure it says, and when I look up, behind a man just turning away from me, one hand rubbing the back of his neck, I catch a glimpse of a woman hastily closing a door. It all happens very fast, but there's no mistaking the expression on her face: she looked scared. I listen to the man walking through the passage, and I'm thinking that the sound of his feet against the floor sings out in a peculiar tune, as if one foot is dragging slightly behind. When I hear a door close I walk back up the stairs and into the empty hallway. To my surprise, the name on the mail slot says *Smith W*, not *Goldstein*, and I add them both to the list of things to remember.

By the time I reach the entrance I am so used to the dark, demanding face that I feel I somehow know him, the Bolshevik on the poster. An old teacher perhaps?

I look out through the glass doors and try to find a clue. Seasonally it must be spring, perhaps the beginning or middle of April, but I couldn't say for certain. *For a dream though, it really is a drab place,* I say to myself and take in the view. Grey and worn down to the bone, it's a concrete workers wet dream. As the unrelenting sour smell keeps eating at my olfactory perception I try hard to read the letters on a huge poster strapped to a distant wall, with one corner flapping loosely in the wind. The word doesn't ring a bell, but I add it to my list, just to make sure.

I decide the cold is the lesser of two evils, and I step outside, directing my steps towards the white pyramid. I walk between apartment buildings, much like the one I just left behind, and everywhere I look, no matter how rundown or unkempt a house appears to be, the one constant is the poster with the staring man. In the distance I hear the whisking beats of a helicopter, and the further I walk, the deeper I am tangled within the chaos of narrow streets. Soon I have completely lost my sense of place, but no matter which way I turn, the pyramid is always in the distance, guiding me like some futuristic lighthouse.

I pass little shop windows littered with trinkets displayed behind grimy glass. A woman stands in the opening of an alley, whispering something my way, smacking her lips faintly. People, ordinary people with aprons, dirty workers' clothes, or jeans full of holes pass in the street, and their very ordinariness strikes me. The uninviting and rather dumb impressions on their faces – are they cruddier versions of people I have met, people I know? Or are they facets of myself? And the streets, the dirty and polluted streets, what do they represent? It's as if a giant wave recently overcame the city, flooding each block before slowly sinking back, leaving a skin of gunk covering everything.

On the out bounds of a larger intersection a vaster space suddenly opens up. A gas station once occupied the corner but now only the canopy and the railings for the pumps remain. In the deserted parking lot stands an old car with the tires missing, and my eyes, which seem to be shamefully awake, catch upon a sticker plastered in the car's back window. Instantly the cobblestone streets and tired, moss-clad houses leaning against each other seem at home. I lift my gaze, and across from where I stand, on the opposite side of the intersection, I spot another sign.

The Chestnut Tree Café is all but empty. Inside are only two other customers, each occupying the two furthest corners. I take a seat at a table in the middle of the room, in a straight line between them, and nod to the waiter behind the bar. I have a look around; a certain daze fills the room, as if the air inside, which seems to have been trapped there forever, has suddenly been stirred. I feel very alert, noticing all details clearly but not for any length of time. Right next to my table, hanging midway up the wall, sits an old mirror. It's the kind you'd see in public toilets at rest stops or, I imagine, in oil-slick factories where burly workers aren't trusted with real glass. It's a dull old thing, oblong in shape, with a reflection so poor I can hardly see my waving hand. It might as well be a dead TV screen.

As I turn around I find the waiter hovering over me. He is clad in a white, starchy jacket, impeccable yet worn, and he busies himself with reaching for something on a tray that he holds at a great distance from the floor, almost pulling away from earth itself.

"What's this?" I ask as he sets a glass down on the table with a faint thud. But as soon as it touches the aged surface the waiter spins around and returns to the bar without a word. I watch as he glides forward, his back fearfully erect, then I turn to my glass. Two things come to mind: one, those were the first words I've uttered in this realm – I wasn't sure they would carry until I tasted their distant echo – and two, if I can speak, can I then also drink? I curiously lift the glass and sniff the colorless liquid; it gives off a sickly, oily smell that reminds me of cough syrup. "When in Rome," I say, and gulp it down. Number two doesn't remain a mystery for long: a burning sensation begins to spread from deep in the hollow of my stomach, and my eyes overflow with tears. *So much for unconsciousness,* I think, and dab at my face with the back of my hand.

Through my newly scorched eyeballs I take another look around the room. The man in the corner to my left sits limp and lifeless, staring down into his glass; both the glass and his stare are empty, and nothing about him makes me curious. On the opposite side of the room there sits a great big man with a lump of greasy red hair on his head, his face swollen and flushed. Once upon he must have been mighty strong, but now his body has swelled on all sides, like dough forgotten on a baker's table. There's really nothing else of interest in the bar, and when I turn back to face the dull mirror, there he is again, the ghost waiter.

It's the same procedure all over again; he holds the tray high, high above his head, reaching, searching atop the plateau, almost on his tippy-toes, for the glass.

"Another one on the house?" I ask, but true to form he is already halfway back to the bar. I down the second glass; this time the sting is only half as bad, but the tears return just the same. It's quite the quaint feeling, the way the room, the entire café actually, seems to be riding on tiny waves. I haven't been drunk in a long time, and now, here I am, sitting in a place woven from threads of imagination, my head spinning from fantasy glasses of spirit.

A murmur begins to build and rise inside me; I can't explain why, but it's a sound that aches to be released. I think of it as a silent humming that wants to escape, tickling my lips faintly as it departs, but as soon as I let it go I loose control of it.

"Aaaaooooouuuu!" I can't recall ever having enjoyed the sound of my own voice so tremendously.

"Aaaaooooouuuu!" It really is a magnificent voice!

I stand up, stagger on the spot, but catch my balance and head over to the bar.

"Aaaaooooouuuu!"

I articulate my lips around each syllable, and the vibrations in the back of my throat bring exquisite pleasure.

"Aaaaooooouuuu! Excuse me, sir," I say and lean across the wooden surface. "What do you call this?"

I hold up my empty glass. The waiter looks at me sheepishly, perhaps wishing I would go away, but I won't have any of it. I'm suddenly enjoying myself tremendously. I wiggle my empty glass at him and raise my eyebrows, waiting for an answer. He is a man with an inconspicuous face: his hair neither dark nor grey, his eyes delivering a neutral stare developed over years of taking orders. But he is no match for me and my murmur.

"Aaaaoooouuuu!"

Indignantly he points at a bottle behind him. I have to lean forward well across the bar to be able to read the label; it's a simple thing, plain and white, and when my eyes wander along the wall I see that every single bottle is tagged with the one and same. Victory Gin is apparently the drink of choice in this dream, and I add it to the list of things I mustn't forget.

The list has now become an intricate game of memory and I search my pockets for a pen and paper to write it all down. With the pen between my lips I try my best to recall all the dream signs, and, in the process, I down my third glass of Victory Gin. Some time later – I can't with certainty say how long I've been at the bar – I am back at my table, a dream within a dream it seems. I open my eyes and, only a couple of tables away, I spot a chessboard with all the pieces set out. I totter over, now quite dizzy, while I call on the stranded redheaded whale.

"A game of chessch, sschailor?" I say, and plunk myself down by the chessboard.

"Letscch do it!" I call out, louder this time, but the man doesn't move.

Instead, here is the waiter again, right by my side, but this time there's no tray in his hand.

"Comrade," his words are strained and careful, as if speaking about private things in a large crowd.

"Can't touch it?" I am shouting now, but it is not an unpleasant feeling, not at all. The vibrations still tickle the back of my throat.

"I can do whatever I want! Thisch is my dream!"

It's an accident when I knock a couple of chess pieces to the floor. I bend down to fetch them, my hand grabbing for the edge of the table for balance, but instead it catches the chessboard, and it all comes crashing down.

I sit silently at the empty table; the waiter is back behind the bar and the chessboard is still on the floor when I hear them come through the door. They walk as one man would, had he four pair of legs, each one following the first one's movement precisely. Their costumes are black, and when they ask me for my papers I realize they are the police.

At first I don't understand what they want.

"Citizen. Citizen. Show us your papers. Show us your papers, citizen."

Their words are distant, yet loud. In front of each of their helmets hangs a reflective visor, and because I can't see their faces they are reduced to four identical copies of the same character. I find them quite annoying, with their loud demanding voices.

"Papers, you say. Here's a paper," and I wave at them nonchalantly with my list, as one would clear the air of an irritating fly. The very next thing I become aware of is my face slamming into the table. I feel my right eyebrow take most of the blow, and everything in the room is abruptly turned on an angle. My gaze is plastered flat, and when the pain in the back of my head wells forward from where it was struck by something very dense, instinctively I know what is next. When I puke, one of them holds me by the hair over the edge. I focus my eyes on the chessboard on the floor and the big black boot standing on it, and I'm not sure what feels worse, the pain in my head or the fact that I can't breathe.

I wake up in a clutter-free room with minimal furnishing. All I see, as I open my eyes, is an empty table with an empty chair, and on the wall the same type of dim, old mirror that was in the café. The room is completely white, and a cold light cuts down from a source I can't focus on long enough to identify. I hear the door move and a man wearing a trim black coverall appears and takes a seat on the other side of the table. He pushes his spectacles up with the tip of his finger – his movements are very precise – and he begins reading aloud from a paper without once acknowledging my existence.

"*1984, A Clockwork Orange, A Farewell to Arms, A Handful of Dust, A Passage to India, A Portrait of the Artist as a Young Man, Absalom, Absalom!, All the King's Men, An American Tragedy, Animal Farm, Anna Karenina.*" He stops, puts a finger on the paper and looks up at me. There is no movement in his face; it's as if he doesn't really see me, as if he were cut in stone.

"I could go on," he says, and I watch lips, straight as tightly twined ropes, mechanically open and close.

"These are all books that don't exist. Not anymore."

He adds the last part with gravitas, casting the sentence in cement.

"But the books are only a minor offence compared to this!" He's picked up the paper, flipped it over to the other side, and as he slams it down on the table in front of me, instinctively I know what it's about. It's my list of things to remember. My dream signs. I read the words scribbled down in a drunken haze at the café: *Big Brother is watching you, Goldstein, Ingsoc, Smith W., Victory Gin.*

"Now, there are several ways we can go about doing this and they will all get us where we want to go. I will ask you once. Where is Goldstein?"

I look at the motionless face with dread, not because of the empty threat, but because already am I very tired of it. I want to go back, back to my desk, even back to my book. This dream has run its course. I'm tired of keeping my eyes open, looking for clues that only muddle what little clarity I have.

"Goldstein sat two rows in front of me in high school, but I doubt he has anything to do with the book I'm trying to write," I say. "Can you take me back now?"

My voice seems to come from out of nowhere – perhaps it's the white ceramic tiles that cover the walls – and I realize I do sound tired.

The very moment I finish the sentence the man snaps up from his chair and hurries out of the room. Before the steel door swings shut I hear the words *This one next* through the closing crack. Seconds later, two uniformed guards enter and lift me brusquely from the chair. I don't struggle as they drag me from the room and herd me through a long corridor, walking behind and to each side of me. The one on my left is thin and wiry, with strong arms that feel more like steel pistons than limbs as he prods my shoulder onward. The other guard is shorter and of stocky build. He twists his body with every step: right arm, right leg, then over to the left, spinning back and forth on his own axle. He reminds me of someone I know, and only as we stop our march halfway down the corridor do I remember who; it's my Aunt Eliza's husband. I search my brain for his name, but too late do I call out, and my "Hey George!" gets stuck inside the room, trapped behind yet another door.

I couldn't say how, but I think they are all the same, the uniformed men, because another one with thin lips and a trim black coverall is already here waiting for me. He motions for me to lie down on a stretcherlike thing. *So, this is the way back,* I think, but I keep my mouth shut. I do feel very tired and gladly get on my back. I don't say a word, not even when some sort of shackles pin my arms and legs down, or when the man lays a strap across my forehead and tightens it until I couldn't move even if I wanted to. All I care about is to close my eyes and fall back awake.

"This goes up to one hundred."

The man's voice sounds soothing behind my eyelids, the voice of a teacher or an instructing father. Slowly, I feel myself begin to drift.

"But I'll start at thirty-five."

35, 35, 35, 35. The number reverberates in my head, helplessly stuck in the same track, while my chest heaves upwards in violent convulsions. The pain that grips my spine is the worst I have ever experienced. It feels torn in all directions, and the fear that it will snap any second, leaving me motionless for life, plasters itself inside my skull. *35, 35, 35, 35, 35.* It stops there, on the last 35, and my body goes limp upon the stretcher. Sweat trickles down my chest; I can feel the drops fall off to the side when they reach my stomach, and when I gaze down I see the thin-lipped man. He is clutching some sort of mechanism in his hand, his fingers gripping a dial.

"Now," he begins, his voice smooth and colorless, without even the slightest hint of compassion, "anyone for forty-five? Forty-five for Goldstein?"

For the second time I cramp up in an arch, leading with my chest, as the intense pain claws at me. I can't say for how long I'm in the grips of terror, but in a spasm of pain I must have ripped my arm and head loose, for the convulsions seize the moment the man tumbles to the floor. I sit halfway up, as far as my one still fastened arm allows me to, my clenched, trembling fist hanging in the air. What just happened? What is this machine? Where am I? It doesn't matter. All I really care about is that the pain is gone. Never before have I felt something so physical, dream or no dream. I try to collect myself, but when the man on the floor starts to moan and stir I decide it's time to leave. Time to leave these corridors and white-tiled rooms, and go back to where it all started, back to Victory Mansions. Back to ground zero. With shaking hands I unbelt myself and stand up. I'm rather careless when I open the door, I don't think it matters, but when the two guards come charging down the corridor, I have no choice but to set off running.

I run through what seems to be a floor of nothing but corridors, a mazelike warren doubling back on itself, each one leading to another. Just as I am dreading that I'm forever stuck in a perpetual chase, I throw myself at a door and find a stair that I fly down, hardly touching the steps. I keep going; the sound of heavy boots pound above and behind me, and when I fling myself against the Do Not Enter sign across yet another door, I pray for it to open. I run along a narrow bridge with a floor made of netted wire; I listen for the boots but can't hear anything other than a distant hissing. It's hot, so hot that drops of sweat fall from my face and disappear through the metal grid beneath me, but I never stop moving. When I reach the other end of the bridge I can hear the boots again.

Isn't it a fact that you wake just before the monster sinks his fangs into you? That you simply have to face it in order for it to go away? I hear the boots closing in, and I walk slowly towards the only door before me. The heat has grown stronger and I am soaked in sweat, but what's worse, I'm almost certain that the hissing is coming from the other side of it. But there's nowhere else to go. I tell myself that I just have to face it for a second, then I'll be back in the library. *Everything is going to be ok.* When I can't wait any longer, when the sound of boots are right behind me, I push open the door and step inside.

I'm in hell. Fire, all around me is fire. The entire floor, except the narrow walkway along the wall on which I'm standing, is a pit of fire the size of an Olympic swimming pool. The heat is a wall in my face, and where I am it is just barely tolerable. Loose papers rain down from a gaping black hole that seems to continue upward forever, and just before they reach the flames, they disintegrate in a silent *poof*. Nothing but fine black dust ever reaches the fire. I carefully begin to sneak my feat out along the ridge, but on the shores of this great fire I have all but forgotten about the guards, and as they push open the door it hits me in the back, and with a scream I dive headfirst into the flames.

2

I open my eyes and the first things I see are books: tightly packed, clothbound books that reach from the floor to well above my head. I track the shelves in both directions until the corridor bends, and all that occupies the space are the two long rows. I'm back. Thank God, I'm back at the library.

I walk down the aisle, so happy that I whistle along to the soft tapping of my feet. I can hardly wait to see good old Harry with his fierce cloud of hair – I am even excited to see Mrs. Hardgrave again. I turn left at the history section and continue down another aisle, but where I want there to be – and there should be – a reception desk, there isn't one. Why would Mr. Krista have the desk moved? Now that I think of it, the layout of the aisles is different too, and the ceiling has been covered in squares of some sort of temporary plating with a dull finish. I make an attempt to regain my bearings; I start upstairs towards my private office but – and I can't even begin to understand how – the stairs have moved as well! Standing at the bottom step, I sense an explanation slowly seeping into me. Walls have been moved, structures restructured – the entire floor plan is totally reorganized. It's really only the books that are the same. Then I understand; I'm not back at the library at all. I am someplace else entirely.

I stand in the place where I first opened my eyes. I remember falling from a great height, my stomach a momentary knot of surprise. I try to do it again. I close my eyes and think of the evil machine, the guards chasing me through the corridors of that hauntingly septic building without windows, and as I fall into the pit of flames I jump straight up, as high as I can... The sound of steps are coming down the aisle, tired feet shuffling forward across the floor. I open my eyes.

"Excuse me," the old man says as he sidles up right next to me and scans the shelf before us.

His eyes move from side to side behind his glasses, before he leans forward and reaches for a book. I manage to catch the title – *Elementary Crystallography* – and as he turns and begins shuffling back towards where he came from, I follow.

"Excuse me," I say. "What happened to the library that used to be here?"

I follow him through the aisles and fire question upon question at him, but the old man remains silent. As if *I'm* not real. He picks up two more books, *The Miracle of the Snowflake* and *The Rhombohedral System*, and when I reprimand him for touching the books he pretends not to hear me.

"We're not supposed to touch them." I say again, but even I hear that my voice is far from authorative. I am simply a lost puppy, nervously tagging along.

Outside it's dark and cold, and I follow behind the man, down the stone steps of the library and out along the street. I look around, but it's hard to say, in the blackness. The surroundings, the dark silhouettes, strike a chord in me; even the man seems familiar in a way, but I can't put my finger on it.

I glance at the sign as we turn the corner onto a narrower street: Boothby Avenue. The trees on each side are featureless creatures that bend and sway in the wind, and behind them buildings erupt solid and silent against the night. Ahead, streetlights drop bubbles of golden reality every fifty steps or so. We haven't walked for but a few minutes when the man suddenly stops. There's trouble up ahead; four men have appeared and are now blocking the way. I recall the feeling of being at the mercy of that horrific machine, and with my heart racing I leap to the side and crouch behind a streetlight. I sense it coming even before one of them snatches the books from under the old man's arm.

Only a few words ring out loud enough for me to make out.

"...excellent...filthy...brother..."

Then there's the old man's voice; it carries well through the night: "Those aren't mine! Those are the property of the municipality!" The four men pull at the books, ripping them to pieces, while the old man cries.

I stay low, peeking out from behind the lamppost at loose bits of paper flying through the sky, and I marvel at the feeling of reality; the air, the sounds, my own heart beating beneath my shirt. Things move fast and suddenly the four have pinned the poor man to the ground, a guttural moan pleading "enough" emitting from their midst. I can only make out the thugs standing above him, pulling at loose garments, moving in and out, tearing into their prey. For every punch and kick the feeling that I should stand up and stop it grows stronger. I am one hair from thrusting myself from behind my cover when something peculiar happens: I remember.

I suddenly recognize the dancing, kicking and laughing men that are wearing what was described as "the height of fashion": black tights cover their legs to above the crotch, and underneath some sort of cup, similar to what hockey players use, and on top waist-length jackets with bulging shoulders and white cravats that make them look like defectors from some visiting dance group. I step out from behind the lamppost, and begin walking towards them.

"Old MacDonald had a farm, EE–I–EE–I–O. And on that farm he had a cow, EE–I–EE–I–O. With a MOO MOO here and a MOO MOO there, here a MOO, there a MOO, everywhere a MOO MOO. Old MacDonald had a farm, EE–I–EE–I–O." I sing in a calm and soothing voice, and when I'm on the last line I've reached the group. Nobody says a word. The old man looks up at me. His spectacles lay crushed beside him, and his breathing is hard. But nobody says a thing. It's the big one who breaks the silence.

"I like a bit of music myself," he says earnestly.

As if the big ones words were the signal he'd been waiting for, the old man claws together his clothes, which lay strewn across the path; all he is wearing is his long underwear, and he gets up and begins staggering off. We watch him in silence, and as he disappears into the night I'm beginning to think that I've made a terrible mistake. A, the leader, although a full minute too slow, lightly elbows the big one in the gut and resumes the center of attention.

"Appy-polly-loggies, little brother. Excuse the big one, he is a tiddle-taddle reverse." They are strange words, a children's language in which gaps are filled with made-up sounds. The four of them eye me up and down, and whisper amongst each other like a group of schoolgirls. *If they come for me I'll turn around and run towards the library*, I think. I'm quite taken by surprise when A takes a step forward and puts a friendly hand on my shoulder.

"Hopalong, little brother, I'll viddie you something that will make your glockers drop."

The four of them hum and sing along to a song I've never heard before and soon we arrive at a bar called the Duke of New York. They leave me outside for a few minutes and I stand looking at my hand, the grooves in my palm, and silently count seconds as they pass. But do they, pass? Everything seems so real, the entire setup, and when they return we continue. I'm not sure how long we walk: I'm the curious trophy along for the ride, I understand as much, for they cast shy looks at me time and again. Then we come upon a street called Attlee Avenue and walk along it for about a mile, and outside a tobacco shop we stop again and they all put masks on.

"Sorry, little brother, no maskies for yous," and while three of them walk inside the one wearing an Elvis mask waits with me outside.

I hear glass breaking and the crash of something tumbling over. There's movement in the windows as the drapes are ripped off, and soon enough everybody comes out and we stand on the street just outside the tobacco shop, the three of them occupied with cleaning the big one up. They use the ends of their shirts to remove stains from his face, straightening out his cravat, as if he was nothing but a giant baby. Then we set off walking again. I can't for my life remember that it was this much walking.

The city – we are somehow in the future, but things are not modern and shiny, quite the opposite – looks weary and rundown. The brick buildings we pass look like the brick buildings on the outskirts of any large metropolitan, with featureless warehouses and apartment blocks of milk-carton anonymity. *Perhaps this was once the future*, I think.

Eventually we arrive at what looks to be some sort of power plant. Large tubes rise towards the sky, where they become pudgy giants in the night, and between buildings run steel walkways ten feet from the ground, almost urging you to play a game of tag.

Only as they step out from the very darkest shadows of a cement block building, and A pulls a knife and the big one starts swinging a bike chain, do I remember the gang.

"Oh, Billyboy, we've come to offer you a real horror-show of a penalty." A nearly sings his threat to the group of men opposite us, and they waste no time replying. As if on a signal they charge, and A and the boys explode out of the blocks, the two masses of flesh and blood colliding in the middle. It's an ugly fight: knife blades catch a twinkle from a desolate light on one of the tubes above and glimmer in the night, and the big one's chain whines like a cat from hell as it cuts through the darkness.

I stay low and retreat from the howling and guffawing, and when the sirens fill the air from somewhere not too distant, I turn around and run.

I've run through the plant, away from the sirens and the fighting, and further into the industrial maze. The darkness is nearly complete in places, but across a deserted lot, under a bush that's grown tall as a tree, there shines a light. It's a fire, burning bright and red in an old, beat-up oil barrel. I gaze carefully into the surrounding darkness; my sweat is beginning to cool and I feel a chill run down my spine.

"Hello?" I say, ready to bolt at the slightest sign of threat.

"Hello?" I call again, and when there's no answer I carefully step up to the burning pit with my hands outstretched.

"Don't be shy. Come a little closer." The voice comes as a total surprise, and my heart immediately sets off on a violent sprint. With the thumping heavy as a jackhammer inside my chest I search all around me – I even look up: the sky is fading from darkness into a dark blue, and tiny sparks rise from the barrel like rain falling in the wrong direction. But nowhere around is there another living soul.

"Down here, you doddery veck."

I follow the direction of the voice, and there it is, a face.

The opening of the barrel has formed itself into a skull, where the licking flames is the flesh, and in the middle of it there's a dark and flameless circle, the mouth from which the words arise.

"My dear Jonathan. What a coincidence to see you here." The flames aside, it's the tone of voice that gives him away. Koob.

It seems like ages ago that I fell asleep on my mattress in the library, and I dare not waste another second.

"I'm ready to go back now," I say in a gulp of air, and I take it for granted that he will understand. He is, after all, my genie. But instead a wild laughter roars from the fire. The guffaw is almost primitive, the ho-ho-ho's barking from the steel tube so violent that the entire barrel starts to shake and wobble, sending a small cloud of glowing nettles into the air.

"Go back? Ha-ha, you slay me, Jonathan! You really do."

There's another outburst before the voice composes itself, breathing heavily while it speaks.

"I think I owe you an explanation, youngen. You see, there are only two ways to call upon me. One is for the aid of the creator, the other as the fierce protector. When you crossed the line, guess what I came as? That's right, and now you must pay the price. The toll of the road. Cross the bridge of good and evil, and all that."

My mind scrambles.

"I apologize for the books," I say in an earnest voice, and I really do mean it. Burning them was unforgivable. "But I'll make it up to you. I promise to replace each and every one of them. But can we talk about it back at the library? Can I please wake up now?"

Another roar of laughter echoes from within the barrel, but this time it doesn't last long enough to set it swaying.

"You ignorant fool!" the voice bellows. "This is not a dream. This is your life!"

With that, a puff of smoke and glowing bits of ash rise into the air; it's a dragon's breath, and I feel my skin sting where it hits.

"You are in the books now, Jonathan," the voice continues, "and there's only one way out."

I have no idea what he is talking about. What does he mean "in the books"?

"The moment you burned those books, I had no choice but to doom you. And now you must make the journey."

"The journey?" I repeat mechanically.

"Yes, the journey through the land of burned pages. You've already done two," Koob adds in an encouraging tone. "I don't have all night, so listen carefully. There are certain rules you have to follow. Rule number one: you have to spend one day in each of the hundred books to be free. Rule number two: you must not stay *longer* than twenty-four hours in each place. This is very important. Rule number three: at the end of each day you will have to find a fire, and it will take you across to the next story. Rule number four:..."

I stop listening. The only thing I can hear is the fire itself, and the soft flapping of flames licking the wind.

"What happens if I stay longer?" I interrupt, still clinging desperately to my red ribbon, trying hard to imagine myself opening my eyes and seeing the cold, dark fireplace in my office.

"Then you stay where you are, locked inside the story," the voice says, and it's a serious face that now looks up at me. "Forever."

It's too much to grasp at once. I feel dizzy; everything is spinning – the sky, the stars, the deserted lot – it whirls round and round, a mishmash of impressions, and finally my balance gives. I feel myself fall and the last thing I hear before it all goes black is my own scream as I dive headfirst into the barrel.

3

It's funny, really, how we all thought it would be the water, but instead it turned out to be the trees.

This was how it began. Those were the first words of the last book in the world.

I'd thought both long and hard about which they should be – believe me, I had – but with time ticking and the pressure from everyone around me building, the only conclusion I had reached was that, when expected to deliver, I was able to come up with nothing. Nil. Zilch. Diddly-squat. The big 0. My mind became a blank slate, a dust-smeared chalkboard, an empty plastic bag – take your pick – and finally I decided I was giving up any grand aspirations that may have been looming there from the beginning. Finally the *size* of the mountain was no longer what was important. All I cared about at this point was to climb any dirt-speckled mound or grassy knoll with enough elevation to earn me the diploma, and get it over with.

All of you present right now know what I'm talking about, but for those who are yet too young, or who are still but a probability somewhere out in the universe, allow me to start from the beginning. There are certain things you need to understand.

First of all, allow me to introduce myself. My name is Jonathan Butter. I could tell you about the whats, hows and whens of my life, the ordinary twists and turns, but none of that is important. What's important is to know that there's nothing special about me. I am the yardstick of mediocrity, the master of convention and ordinarity, your typical run-of-the-mill, salt-of-the-earth, average kind of Joe. My point is, I could have been you. So how did I end up here, in this place where time stands still? Well, let me begin by telling you about my house.

Actually, in my life there were two: the house where I worked and the house where I lived. Both were constructed of red brick over a hundred years old, with walls stacked so thick and sturdy that when you were inside it was completely quiet. Only very loud noises managed to pass through the masonry. Inside it was like the outside world didn't exist. Yet in one principal matter, both were utterly different: where I lived I couldn't stand that silence, but where I worked I embraced it. Besides the obvious reason, that's why I started sleeping at my office.

I'm not sure exactly when it started. I suppose, as with all things, it started when we struck those first flints together and learned to master the spark. I do, however, know for certain when I first heard about it. It was in sixth grade, during a geography class. We talked about the rain forests, how they were the lungs of the world, and I remember that it seemed strange to my pubertal mind to have body parts thus scattered all across the globe, and I couldn't quite figure out where the rest of the body was. Then, ten years ago, the

Forest Party was founded. At first it was only an ant among other ants, all trying hard to make their voices heard. None, however, had any real power. Swarming the anthill were the Air Party, the Information Party, the Transportation Party, and of course the Water Party. They all had their glory days, but when it had spread far enough for the trees around the big cities to die and fall to the ground – when it could no longer be ignored by the ordinary man – that's when the Forest Party exploded. But by then it was too late. All we could do then was watch them die.

If you are reading this and, looking out a window, you can see a tree, or hear the wind sweep through its branches and rustle its leaves, then the program has worked and this might not be the last book after all. But if you look out your window and see only buildings, or a plain of dirt and patches of grass, with nothing leafy sprouting towards the sky, then we are still trying. For either of you, in order to remember and to understand, this is what happened.

Ten years ago, the Forest Party had already warned us about it. Of course, at that time nobody really knew: it was just a single cry for help among many other cries. People had said something of the sort throughout the century, but there are so many people saying so many things that we needed *proof* to back it up.

Proof came during the Forest Party's fifth year. It was indisputable: the trees of the world were dying. At a rapid pace, forest after forest disintegrated until the green areas of maps turned brown. Thinking that united we would be stronger, the world powers joined forces against this invisible enemy, but neither leading scientists nor military researchers nor any biologist could explain it. By the Forest Party's ninth year less than one percent of the world's trees remained.

As I write this there are still some patches of forest scattered about in the world. (When I look out the window, from my room on the second floor at the hospital, you'd think that the world was back to normal again; I see lots of trees – the apple orchard in the park below, a mat of dark green pine trees covering the mountain sides in the distance – but none of them are really there.) All are heavily guarded, some surrounded by high walls, others covered completely by domes. Not a single tree has been harvested the last five years. The few left are there for research purposes only, in the hopes of one day rebuilding the world, twig by twig, leaf by leaf.

Even though many think that the forest is gone forever and what we fight so hard to keep alive is only a curious keepsake of the past, some still believe. About half of us do, the polls said on TV (sadly, there's no TV here), and I count myself as one of them. I really don't have a good reason to, but I still do. The alternative is just too depressing.

There's that old expression, that we don't miss what we have until it's gone. Many things came from trees, so many I wouldn't even have known to miss them before they were no longer here. I won't bore you with a list because – and that's the irony of it all – lists are one of those very things. A blank sheet of paper, a yellow Post-it note, a page torn from a notebook, an old envelope, the corner of a newspaper. That's the reason I'm here. Simply put, without trees there's no paper, and without paper there are no books.

It makes me think of that other old expression, you can't see the forest for the trees. It was a popular joke for a while, when it all started, but it's been a long time since I last heard it.

It first became noticeable in bookstores. Prices surged, and books soon became a luxury item. Everything was available digitally anyway, most people reasoned, so why buy expensive paper books? Then there were the connoisseurs, the ones who couldn't make themselves pick up a Kindle, an iPad, or a Sony Reader and slide through the electronic pages. Books are tangible, they smell, they rasp your fingers, they make a certain sound as pages are turned. They are physical anchors in an increasingly artificial world. As forest after forest died, books became – well, not literally, but well close to it – worth their weight in gold.

Conflicts, some might even call them wars, broke out across the world on account of paper. Like oil, it became both prisoner and jailer of world peace, and it wasn't long before all nations came together and agreed upon a plan. It worked: conflicts were smothered and the paper trade regulated, but the trees kept dying. Slowly, societies adapted to the new rules of life. Books left schools altogether, goods were packed in plastic and foam, and soon even a simple piece of paper, especially a blank one, neared the status of a collectible.

But among the rulers – all of whom had grown up amongst bookshelves stocked with volumes of words and pictures, who had been sent off to dreamland by their favorite chartaceous fairy tales, and who had inhaled (as much physically as mentally) from between the covers the things that had made them into the women and men they were today – there was a yearning for something more. To be able to say, *This is the last piece we will ever see, take care of it*, was somehow hugely different from just waking up one day and realizing it was all gone. Preparation for the end, I suppose that's what we all wish for. One last moment, then you can take us away. And that's how it happened. That's what you are reading. The last book in the world.

There was a competition. It spanned the globe, and the rules, in order to pull the worst weeds, were both intricate and abundant. Still, we were some twenty-seven million applicants. One of the requirements was that you had to, in some way, shape, or form, work with books. Was it a slip-up from the very start? Should the rules have been more specific? Would I have applied if they had been? All I know is that the loose description meant that you could be either an already published author or a book-industry executive, but it also made the factory workers in printing houses eligible.

I first read about it in an online library magazine. The writer encouraged librarians to enter the competition, "To make a stand for our lofty trade," as he so eloquently put it. Obviously, I never thought I would win, and at the time I wasn't sure how it happened. It was only afterward that I learned – and there's been much debate around this – it was more of a lottery than an actual competition. I suspect, and this has been confirmed in somewhat fuzzy statements from anonymous members of the board, that the one thousand words we each submitted weren't even read.

In all honesty, twenty-seven million applicants times one thousand equals twenty-seven *billion* words. How can a board the size of the UN be expected to read twenty-seven billion words? I certainly know – I have never fooled myself – that there are thousands, more likely hundreds of thousands, of writers out in the world who are more accomplished than me in every way you can measure. It really should have been one of them. What I'm trying to say is, I wish I had never won.

I might as well be honest with you from the start, for I'll get no second chance. The truth is that if I could have passed this honor on, this honor that has transformed into a curse, I would have. But I'm afraid it was impossible. Believe me, I tried to persuade the board that they'd made a grave mistake, but they refused to listen. Too much was riding on this to start diverting from the rules. They made it very clear that, although the world is not about paper alone, right now paper is the glue that keeps it united. So, no matter how reluctant and apprehensive I felt, I had to come to terms with my role in this. It was a great burden to carry – it still is – and I'm not sure if I will ever finish in time, let alone make it back. All I know is that I have no choice but to push forward. May the world's readers have mercy on me.

4

Twenty-four hours. When I wake up I'm on my back in the middle of a field, with Koob's words echoing in my head. The field is a muddy square where nothing grows, and above me, strange, whistling creatures jet through the air. I close my eyes again and think of my mattress, the fireplace, Mr. Krista, the library, and Johanna; I drag them out and hold them to the light, and just as I am about to reach out and touch them, the images shatter with a loud *bang*. The ground has not finished shaking before the next *bang* again sets it in motion, and I am forced to see the shards of memory disappear into the light.

The field, I discover as I first crawl, then crab-walk, and eventually straighten out into an upright walk, isn't the newly plowed plot I first thought it to be, but rather a crater of overturned dirt. All around me are similar craters, like scars on the face of some giant, acne-ridden man, and to my surprise new craters burst open in steady intervals. I can't say if the whistling precedes the explosion or if it is something that lingers after – my senses are slow to come back, from where I'm not sure, but eventually the feeling of just waking up from a long, deep sleep leaves me fully awake. I reach the edge of the field, where the whistling and the loud bangs aren't quite so overbearing, and in a matter of minutes the noise ceases completely and the whole land falls into a deep silence.

At the end of the world I can see mountains rise high and mighty. I set off towards them, away from the dimpled field, and my steps soon take me to where a forest begins. At the base of the forest – *Chestnut forest*, the words rise to the surface unbidden – further down in the valley, I spot a stream that cuts cool and silvery through the green. Where the stream turns slightly larger pools form where, I imagine, the water isn't flowing, only twirling around slowly. White boulders line its edge, boulders that from up here on the plateau look no bigger than marbles.

I walk a path leading down a slope, and I study the leaves; thick and very green, they seem tough as hide, and the air, the air is so clear and fresh that it slips in and out of my lungs with great ease. *Perhaps this is a sign it is ending.* I remember thinking this, filled with a feeling of serenity and, despite it all, a surprisingly abyssal calm. I can hardly belive it now, looking back, that I in the midst of chaos and mystery, in the forest, the forest that wasn't really a forest, accepted my place without even putting up a fight. As if I had already submitted my sanity to a jar of little blue pills.

I search the valley below for any indication of life. The silence is heavy, only when I pass a fallen tree covered in sprays of moss, and a pigeon explodes into motion and disappears between the branches, does the landscape momentarily fill with life. Soon after, as the vegetation clears, I spot the camp about a quarter mile down.

"Hez here, hez here! Signor, pleeez come wiz me."

The man, musky and dark, appears from out of nowhere as soon as I step from the path and onto the valley floor. He is wearing a soldier's uniform made from brown, thickly woven cloth, and a helmet that's at least two sizes too big for his head. From under the helmet black locks of hair curl upwards, as if holding it in place.

"Signor, pleeez come wiz me," the soldier pleads and proceeds to take me under the arm. I'm confused and let him lead the way.

We don't have to walk far before we've arrived in the middle of a large camp. From above, up on the plateau, I could never have guessed there was a hutment of this size down below, thanks in large to it's superb location; it sits hidden around a bend in the landscape, nestled behind a tongue of rising hills. Big guns on wheels stand in attentive rows, while several trucks and a Jeep are parked in disorderly scatters around them. Grey tents spring from the ground that was once, I presume, covered in grass, but is now nothing but a sandy pit. I think we are headed for the largest of three in a row, but the soldier keeps us moving, past high piles of army-green boxes bearing the text *Explosives*, and past groups of men smoking, leaning against rifles, or playing cards on the ground. Where the sandy pit runs out of sand and the grass still thrives, the soldier stops before a dugout on the other side of a mound and lifts the tarp so I can step inside.

"Signor, write a story about me!" "And me, Signor. Write about how I kill many enemies!" "Write how we stay in the dirt here for a long time to save our sisters from the

Austrians. Say we are heroes. How we eat like pigs and drink only one bottle of wine a week!" "Write about me, I am Luchetti! And me, I am Pupparo! I am Garone! Pennachi! Constantino!"

They were five men in the dugout, plus the man who brought me there.

"What is your name?" I ask him, more because I feel it is expected from me, than any real curiosity on my part.

"Petraglia," the man says, "but you don't have to write about me. I haven't killed any Austrians yet."

The group eyes me expectantly, and I'm not sure what to do or say. I fidget with my hands, and as I slip them inside my pants pockets I feel the paper there.

"What is your name, Mr. Reporter?"

I understand at once. A wartime journalist who visits the front, ends up in battle or is taken prisoner by the enemy, and in the end manages to pull off a heroic stunt, win the battle, and save himself so he can get his article. I know it's a movie but can't pin the title down.

"Jonathan," I say, "Jonathan Butter, and I write for the *New Library Times*."

After the initial introductions I make a few notes on the back of the paper. I ask questions about the war – I have no idea which it is – and I scribble the answers down. One man comes back, I think it is Pennachi, carrying a large pot, with a jug of wine stuck under his arm. We gather around it: freshly cooked pasta with butter that is still melting from a big yellow glob. Pennachi produces a cheese the size of two fists from his coat pocket, and he crumbles it over the pasta before everyone digs in with their forks. I don't have a fork, but Luchetti hands me a spare one, and we each take turns lifting spaghetti straight up from the pot and sucking it in with a slurping sound. The jug of wine is passed around: it's sour and harsh, but everyone seems happy to get a taste, and I don't make a face. Everyone is quiet as we eat, pasta is lifted high up in the air, the sucking and the slurping, and the passing of the wine bottle from mouth to mouth the only sound I hear. When the pot is empty, everyone leans back, relaxed and satisfied. Someone burps, and Garone looks at me seriously and asks, "How is your country like?"

I'm just about to think up a great answer that will give them something to imagine for weeks when I hear the *chuh-chuh-chuh-chuh*. Then there is a flash, as if we've stepped onto the red carpet at a movie premiere, and a mighty roar that goes from one ear to the other in a hot second, and then all the air is pulled from my lungs and no matter how hard I try, nowhere around me is there any new to suck down.

I am not passed out; I hear machine gun smatter from a distance and right next to me, someone is crying out, "Mama mia! Oh mama mia!" over and over again. Then I do faint, because the next thing I know I am on a stretcher in the back of a truck. We traverse one ridge after another, at least that's how it feels in the darkness, and I know that around me are other stretchers, for I hear mumbles and the scrapings of steel against the floor every time the truck jerks. We ride like this for some time – perhaps it's hours, then maybe it's only twenty minutes – and eventually we stop and the tarp on the side of the truck is slung over the roof and a wave of light wells inside and over us. I am carried by strong hands to the second floor of a house I later learn is a hospital and carefully transferred from the stretcher to a bed in an almost empty room. At some point the doctor comes in, and when he touches my head I don't feel any pain, only a sort of numbness, and when he is done a nurse wraps me up in white gauze, only down to my eyebrows, leaving me to see the day creeping into evening through the windows. After bringing me some water and checking on me twice the evening has turned to night, and the nurse leaves me alone. As if dark creatures in a glass aquarium I watch bats chase insects in the night, but only as they pass the luminous moon can I make their silhouettes out. Soon a gang of clouds drag in, making the darkness complete, and I lie back and close my eyes. I try not to think about anything at all.

When I wake up my head hurts something terrible. The world is slightly out of focus and I have no apetite for the food the nurse brings me on a tray. She is very nice, her hair silvery and tightly wound in a bun atop her head. She puffs my pillow and checks my bandage, but the headache she can't do much about. I lay like this the whole first day, trying to keep the world from spinning, and by evening it does and I feel very thirsty. I use the bell connected to the cord to call for a glass of water, and after that my headache eases up and I fall asleep.

In the morning I get out of bed before the nurse has made her first visit and walk over to the window. My head still aches, but it's not that bad. For the first time I see the garden with blossoming fruit trees – a view I eventually will become far too aquainted with – and I decide to go for a walk. I find my clothes in the closet but when I bend forward the headache bites me and the dizziness returns. I sit on the bed and button my pants, and that's when I notice it: the paper. I pull it from my pocket and, like a suspended wave waiting to crash down upon me, the clock starts and it hits me full on. It's *my* paper and they are *my* words, and I know they mean something. My headache doubles, pressing blood through needle thin membranes, causing them to burst and overflow. I get it. I do get it now. *1984.* Orwell. I turn the paper over to the other side, then back, and then back to the other side again. Burgess, Alex and his droogs. I look out through the window, I see the trees, *the trees*, I think, how strange. *I am in Italy and there's a war.* I know there's truth in it; he was in a hospital, something about his legs, and then there was that woman, Catherine.

A fire, I remember that was my only thought, *I have to find a fire.*

The cool outside air stings my nose and makes my eyes water, but it passes after the first few breaths. I walk through a nearly empty town where only a few elderly people are yet up and about, and as I bid them a good morning with a nod, I see a glint in their eyes when they notice the bandage.

The streets are cobblestone and the houses made of large, square-cut rocks, some with tile roofs, others protected by wood shingles. By the looks of it, it's a very old town.

The longer I walk, the more people I see, although at no time are there many people out. It's as if the town has been evacuated, poorly, but nevertheless emptied out in a rush. I have no idea where I'm going – all I know is that I need a fire – and when I chance upon an old lady with a scarf tied around her head and a long piece of bread squeezed under her arm I realize the answer is standing right in front of me.

"Excuse me, Senorita," I say, even though I know it's Spanish. "The bread" – I point at it – "Where can I get some?"

She looks at me, then at my bandage, and I think she must be thinking that I'm crazy. "Explosion. Boom," I say, and point towards the mountains that rise like another world in the distance.

A smile breakes her face in two as she extends the bread in my direction.

"No, no. Where? *Donde esta?*" I say, and sweep my hand around the city.

Finally she understands what I mean, and points towards the church tower that sticks up far above the other roof tops.

The bakery sits on a corner, a stone's throw from the church. It's easy to find – the smell of freshly baked bread hangs deep and sweet about the entire block. When I enter a bell is set in motion above my head, and I listen to the soft jingles slowly die out while a man shuffles forward from the back.

"Signore," he begins, but stops short when he sees my face. "You American?"

"Yes, yes I am!" I say, unable to constrain my excitement.

"Ah, I am so pleased to meet you," he says and begins a story about a relative of his who emigrated to America and started an olive oil company.

I let him talk, even though I feel my seams are bursting from the inside. The man – his name is Giorgio, I later learn – looks to be of the mountain-bred sort: short, stocky, deep-chested, with meaty forearms built great by the moving of miles of dough. His hair is a natural black, but as everything in his shop, and so also the compact moustache under his nose, it is covered in a thin layer of flour, rendering him almost transparent. A bakery ghost.

"Sorry, signore, sorry for talking," Giorgio says and spreads his hands in an apologetic gesture, finally finished with his story. "What can I get you?"

Suddenly I am nervous. My bandage feels very tightly wound, and the heat in the bakery has become overwhelming. I stick one finger up the side of the gauze and relieve my itch before I propose my question: "May I… is it possible... could I…" I pause, take a breath, and let it out. "I would really appreciate if I could just take a look at your fire." The baker stares back at me, motionless. I have this notion that he, any second, will explode in anger, take me for a loon and run me out of his shop, chasing after me with stale loaves of bread. But just as I'm about to begin backing towards the door, his ghostly face bends into a smile, and he holds an inviting hand out for me while lifting up a section of the counter with the other. *Come see the fire.*

We stand in front of the baker's oven, and this time it really does look like a mouth: the chimney is large and wide; it reaches down from the ceiling in a mushroom-shaped hat, the hollow opening creating a toothless, grinning gape. The baker tells me all about the oven and the bread he bakes in it. He says that the fire has been burning for a hundred years straight, "or so the story goes," he adds and wiggles his eyebrows.

He is interrupted by the bell up front, and he shuffles out to take care of his customers. I know I have to hurry, but I don't know the first thing about how to call upon him. Was there a rhyme or a certain way I should touch the oven? After a few moments of silent debate I simply lean forward, as far as I dare into the mouth, until the blistering heat stops me just as effectively as any wall. I stare into the flames.

"Koob?" I whisper. "Are you there?" Coals and not-yet-consumed logs of real wood are lodged in the back, and the flames dance above them gingerly, as if teasing me. But they are doing no such thing; I can see straight away that the fire isn't alive. Koob isn't there, and I pull back my scorched head, thus beginning my imprisonment.

5

I began from home. On the southwest side of a perfectly square park (needless to say, treeless) my old house sat like a stranded ship. I say that because I couldn't help but feel as if it didn't really belong there, the way it squirmed between the other houses, perhaps having once tried hard to wiggle out, but now old and tired, simply leaning against the neighboring walls in silent defeat. On this stranded vessel, the stair leading up to the second floor and my apartment careened sharply to one side, so much that anyone who came here for the first time thought they had entered a funhouse. At least, that's how one reporter put it. She told me she expected to find mirrors that threw her body out of proportion and a kitchen table glued to the ceiling.

The wooden floor in my living room suffered from the same affliction, and a ball placed on one side would roll to the other without even the slightest push. Regardless, I had a great deal of affection for my house, the way you would for a dog with only three legs. The way we can't always choose where we end up.

There was a whole lot of commotion in the beginning, but they kept that away from me. A car, the same black sedan that brought the official from the board with the news that first day, was always to my service. Through my window I sometimes saw them in the park, the black-coated men, all the same height, each one indistinguishable from the others. They were there to guard me from the press, from the curious public, and, I gather, from one or two angry writers. But from the very beginning I was never able to shake the feeling that they were also my prison guards, posted out there to keep me in. I could go and come as I pleased, but always in the black sedan, and even without looking I knew the black-coated men were all around, securing areas, talking into wrists, melting into the background.

The first time I saw them was when I met Mr. Krista. He was the one they sent to the library that day, and after he became my primary contact. Judging by the way he spoke and the things he said, my guess was that he was closer to sixty years old, but judging by the way he looked I couldn't have said more than forty. It was truly hard to tell. Perhaps you've seen him on TV? He was there that day at the ceremony, together with the rest of the board. A man of average height, with coal-black hair combed thick and wet to the side, not one strand of hair overlapping another.

But it wasn't just his hair; Mr. Krista was perfect in many ways. Take his hands, for example. When I first touched them they were soft and warm, but steady and controlling, as if *they* decided when you were letting go. I really don't know much at all about Mr. Krista; even though I met him countless times.

The things I do know are just guesses and assumptions. Mr. Krista never talked about himself, and cornered by a question, he always elegantly found a way out.

That day I was behind the loan desk. It was a quiet day – as it always was inside the library – and I was keeping busy rearranging cards for the display in the history section. That was all we ever did, displaying books, just like in a museum (There are books here, books you can touch, open, smell and hold against your chin, anything except read – unless you know Italian). Anyway, that day, the outside world suddenly seeped in through the open door, as it does for a moment every time a visitor enters. Except this time the door didn't close. I looked up and saw a black-coated man standing right inside, holding the edge of the door with a black-gloved hand, and I was just about to say something to him regarding the draft when Mr. Krista walked in. Somehow, before he even extended his hand, I knew what it was about.

Everything went so fast. After the initial commotion and ceremonial festivities, I began working from home. Sitting at my desk, overlooking the park, I caressed the keyboard and stared at the newly installed computer. When I tired of that I fingered the hand-bound notebooks flown in from a high-security vault in London, all supplied to me by the board, via Mr. Krista. But I couldn't find it in myself to begin. How could I be expected to? One day I was me with a select few, the next I was part of the collective consciousness. I was in turmoil. Days went by, and I spent them by the desk, drawing doodles in the notebooks and enjoying this rare and luxurious opportunity to waste paper. Occasionally, when I looked up, there they were, the black-coated men moving in the park.

We get a certain something in our heads when we hear it, *The Last Book in the World*. It's a name infused with obligations. I see something different now, but back then I saw a book so sweet and heavy that every single sentence dripped with the nectar of genius. And when you set out to write the greatest book ever written, it does put some undue pressure on you. And that heavy object pressing you down makes you unable to breathe. And when you can't breathe, you can't relax, and when you can't relax, thoughts become frightened birds that fly away the moment you approach them. In short, the magnitude of what I had been chosen to do was sinking in, and I was scared shitless.

All in all, I wasted twelve weeks by the desk in my shipwrecked house. I use that word, *wasted*, for had I only found it in myself to take those first, vital steps across the trecherous beginnings, perhaps I wouldn't be where I am now.

The ugly truth is, back then I had no intention of ever finishing. My plan was simple: to let enough time pass so that when I went back to the board they would realize I could never finish before the deadline, forcing them to pick someone better suited.

I'm not sure what made me change my mind. Well, I do know what changed it, but I couldn't say how she found me. Or where she came from. It was a Sunday, and I'll never forget it.

It was one of those days when everything in the world had slowed down. The sun's rays sort of floated in the wind, instead of jabbing down sharply as usual, and behind each and every one of them a golden streak gently speared the earth.

I was by my desk; I had just finished filling the very last notebook with doodles and sat staring out the window. For once the men in black coats were nowhere to be seen, and, all of the sudden, from the most faraway corner of the path circling the park, a woman cut across the lawn in big strides. And just as I had known what message Mr. Krista would deliver to me that day before he even extended his hand, I knew that the girl was heading for my door.

Her name was Johanna, and it's a mystery how she managed to get past the black-coated men, but she did. For, a short while after I lost sight of her in the window, there came a knock on my door.

I'll always remember the first time I saw her face. I think I would have even if it hadn't been so very beautiful.

Her eyes were a deep chestnut brown and slightly wet, as if the wind had been just a bit too violent, and this one strand of dark hair stuck to her lips – she only noticed when she began speaking.

"How are you?" she said, the tone of her voice as if we were already good friends. I liked her right away.

She walked over to the bed and sat down; she sat very straight, with her knees touching, and while she spoke I noticed how much I'd missed people these last weeks.

Although the library wasn't overflowing with social interaction, there were still the polite phrases of coming and going, the courteous kit that made us all feel connected.

She was concerned about the book, she said, not so much for herself but for me. She said she couldn't imagine the pressure of writing the one book everybody in the world was waiting for, and if it had been her, she would have completely frozen up, unable to think of anything.

From where I was sitting I could see that she had caught a glimpse of the desk, and by the way the rhythm of her words skipped a beat I knew that she had noticed the notebooks. A sudden signal from the phone cut through the room and zipped it shut.

"I should take it," I said apologetically and turned towards the front door, where my jacket hung on the coat rack.

It was Mr. Krista. He called every now and then to see if I needed anything and, I suspect, to check up on my writing. Although never once did he ask me straight out about it. When we hung up and I turned back, Johanna was no longer sitting on the bed.

"Aha, just what I thought," she said and waved one of the notebooks my way.

But there was no harshness or mockery in her voice. It was simply neutral, as if she were commenting on the dealings of underwater species in an aquarium.

Strange as it may sound, I wasn't angry. My secret was out, and what I felt most of all was relief. Finally I could let my guard down. I didn't waste another second and began at once to tell her everything. I told her about how I wanted out, that I had no idea where to start, that I wasn't a great writer – perhaps not even a good writer – and that all I had managed in the twelve weeks so far was to fill a bunch of endangered notebooks with doodles. I vented my fears, and the mere act of saying them out loud helped dim them. It was foolish – in hindsight it was foolish – for this is where a twist in the road grew into a bend.

On that slow-moving day something extraordinary occured, something that would change everything. Johanna's question seemed laced with profound clarity: What were my favorite books? It was impossible to say. I'd read so many – I mean, I was surrounded by them all day long.

"Close your eyes and think of one," she said, and I did.

I thought of one great book, and I kept it in my mind just as I was told, went through it quickly from beginning to end, felt it in my heart again, tasted its flavor and let the emotions take over.

"Now," she began, her soft voice filling the entire room, my entire head, "tell me where the greatness lies."

I never got as far as answering because the question itself unlocked something inside me that held the solution to my problem. A revelation appeared.

"Of course!" I said and opened my eyes.

I took Johanna's hand in mine and said it again.

"Of course."

Why should I search for greatness in my own head when I had it all around me? Lining shelf after shelf, cloth-bound, calf-bound, sewn, stitched and glued, the library was filled with the greatest books ever written. They would tell me what to do. Within them I would find the answer.

A few days later I moved to the library. They cleared out the second-floor office for me to use as my private writing room – they even moved my desk over. Furthermore – and I think this was the work of Mr. Krista – the library was now only open between nine and noon; the rest of the time I had the entire place to myself. And all I said was that I thought I *might* concentrate better at the library.

The talk about greatness, it really got me thinking. I figured that I could take, say, one hundred of the world's greatest books, find the greatness in each one of them, dig it out like a mole on the prowl for succulent worms, and transfer it to my book.

All around me stood the collected sweat and blood of the most brilliant minds in the history of mankind: authors, novelists, scientists, preachers, and gods, who together had spent hundreds of years in front of desks, on benches, or behind bars, squeezing words from their tongues when they wouldn't pour, and filling bucket after overflowing bucket when they did. And this thought that I would use other people's greatness to create my own became so vivvid that I dropped everything else; I put all my money on this one horse of an idea, and I never even tried to put my own words on paper. If I had perhaps none of this would have happened.

My new office was in an old living room. Once upon a time, more than sixty years before I started working there, the building that housed the library was the mayor's residence, and my office the grand salon. Sixty must also have been the number of years since the fireplace had held an actual fire.

It was a great big mouth that sat at the base of the chimney, with decades of old soot hidden behind the whitewashed and toothless hollow.

My desk sat at an angle to the fireplace, facing it and the left side window equally, and beneath my feet was a big Oriental carpet, a behemoth of wool, somewhat old and worn, but with a beautiful pattern. Fantasy animals graced its fantasy forests – it was a scene that one almost wanted to dive into. They say carpets like these tell stories, like a book woven from yarn, and if they hadn't taken years to complete, perhaps I would have been sweating it out by a loom instead of my desk.

I had been issued exactly one year by the board, not a day more, and then my work had be done. A whole world was waiting and, as they say in show business, timing is everything. I had already spent three months by my desk, looking at the park, drawing doodles, then another three weeks getting organized at the library and accepting my purpose in all this. That left me a little less than eight and a half months to complete the book. Correction: to begin the book, and *then* complete it.

Back then that seemed to be an awfully long time to do just the one thing, but was I ever wrong. In a way it's really ironic, for now I have nothing but time.

It was really the list that I was struggling with. The hundred greatest books in the world. How does one decide? I did some research and found a number of lists online. Many magazines and newspapers had compilations of what they considered being the greatest books of all time. Many books appeared on all of the lists, while some were absent from a few, and some lists had books none of the others had. The lists aside, there were also other things to consider. What were the criteria for calling something great? What made a book exceptional? If a certain book was on a list, did that automatically qualify a book of similar scope and perception? Should I compile a list of books that changed the world or simply books that were a good read? Should the lists be books that caused discussions and gave us readers something completely new? Or should it simply be the most widely read works? Is it even possible to compare books to each other? I read the lists over and over, I searched reference books and considered the opinions of literary critics and professors – I even made an attempt at creating my own list, but scrapped it halfway through. I finally realized that I had to compile a list from all other lists and use that as my map.

I began my work the very next day. Every day when I arrived, my office looked exactly the way I left it the day before: if a pen was crossing the bottom tip of a notebook at a certain angle when I left in the evening, it crossed it in the exact same angle when I arrived in the morning. Somehow this was both enticing and intimidating. To feel that I was alone with this, that I was completely free to do what I pleased, but that I must walk alone.

I was prepared to dive headfirst into creation, but automatically the littlest details did their best to unhinge me. My ears trailed off, searching the locality for any sounds; they scanned the room from top to bottom, all the way to the corner by the right side window, where they came up with the faintest hint of a hissing that could be either water rushing through a pipe buried deep within the wall, or simply the sound of the world spinning.

"The list," I said out loud and shook my head, "focus on the list."

An hour later printouts were scattered across my desk. I began by cross-referencing them to find books that were present on all lists, and these I safely transferred onto mine. This took until well after lunch, and the results were sixty-three books already in place.

When I stepped out into the library, it was completely deserted. I knew the black-coated men were right outside and all I had to do to reach them was dial 2 on my phone, but so far the only times I'd had to call upon them were when I wanted to be driven to and from the library. Anything else, I'd dial 1 and Mr. Krista, or his secretary, would answer. But I had everything I needed right here: row upon row of bookshelves filled the big hall, and thousands upon thousands of books, spanning from Greek mythology to the mating habits of bullfrogs, lined their shelves. I walked with determination towards the fiction section, my mind fixed on not leaving until I had excavated my gold nuggets.

Three hours later the list was complete. One hundred of the greatest books in the world. It was invigorating to see them together like that, ten piles of ten books each, all on just the one cart. One could only imagine the sweat and tears that went into their creation, all the brilliant thoughts flowing through the minds of brilliant men and women, and now they had all come together on my book cart.

I kept most of the books on my desk, and the ones that didn't fit I piled atop the mantelpiece. It was early morning and I was all alone. I remember that the silence was light and airy, like a room filled with bubbles, when I picked up the phone and called Mr. Krista.

I had decided that I would go on a camping trip: a hike through the National Park of Literature.

The way I imagined it, when I thought of a writer – at least a great writer – I saw them close the door on the world. Sealing themselves off in a cabin in the middle of nowhere, perhaps near a lake or on top of a mountain, while ordinary life played out down below. There they sat, closer to heaven, dreams, and creation, and they didn't come back until they had found what they were looking for. Neither would I.

The goods arrived late afternoon: a bundle of new notebooks, a roll of pens, a sleeping bag, a mattress, a big bowl of mints, and one of those stress-reliever balls with bulging plastic spikes. There was also a handwritten note from Mr. Krista, saying, "Anything else, just let me know. Good luck, K."

I placed the stress-reliever ball on the left side of my desk and the bowl of mints on the right; I opened up a brand-new notebook, I pulled a pen from the roll, I took a deep breath, and… something was missing.

I sucked on the mint for a second before I opened my eyes, and let the cool mist numb my nostrils. Finally, I was ready.

I sat at my desk until well after ten, but the only time my pen moved was when my hand reached for another mint.

The beginning is treacherous. That first step into darkness... I didn't want to rush it. I decided to sit there until it came naturally, as a visiting friend poking his head through the door.

At midnight, the words still absent, I unrolled my sleeping bag and went to bed on the mattress. The mints had upset my stomach – it burned cold and raw – and I turned to the side, and fell into a restless sleep.

By the next day I had made a decision to take it easy on the mints. I devised a system where only for each page written could I indulge. By lunch time the mints remained untouched.

I still belive all great artists begin this way, not the mints; I don't mean the mints, but the struggle. It's part of the process. Without the pangs of doubt and despair, the right words will shine with their absence. The very words that ache with truth and clarity. You have to give birth to such words. You have to be lost before you can find your way.

I was lost alright. I didn't know in which end to start. I entertained ideas that involved writing about each book, sort of an extended literary critique of the greatest works of fiction ever created. I would analyze characters and plots, sift them through a net until, in the end – if I succeeded – I'd be left with the nuggets of greatness. I also thought about writing about each author, the real protagonists of the famous works, summarising their lives from early childhood to the moments of creation, and from that perspective find the common denominators that spawned greatness. Or the covers, I thought of doing the covers – a written kaleidoscope of the original covers to in turn tell the stories they embraced. Or a decoction of first reviews to show the greatness in the ways they had impacted readers and society. The possibilities were endless. I had all the bricks to build my Taj Mahal – what I didn't have was a form.

Every now and then Harry and Mrs. Hardgrave came by to see me. Good old Harry, it was a bittersweet time for him. Sweet because he'd been promoted to Loan Desk Manager, the position I held prior to my writing engagement, and bitter because the library was now only open three hours a day. I miss him, my redheaded friend with freckles galore. He was the only person I knew that had no problems keeping all the characters in Dostoyevsky's books apart.

My softened heart even has a space reserved for Mrs. Hardgrave. She was of the old-fashioned kind, dry-witted and at times sharp-tongued, but always so subtle that it was only afterwards you realized that you had, in fact, been insulted. She'd been at the library for ages, and in the years I had known her, her appearance hadn't changed one bit. It was as if she every night steeped herself in formaldehyde.

It was actually after one of Mrs. Hardgrave's visits that something was jarred loose in me. "You're in the newspaper, " she said and waived a reader my way. (Newspapers, remember when we used to get them on our doorsteps? That's right children, they tossed one in front of every house, every single day of the week.) I never had any interest in what they wrote about me, but Mrs. Hardgrave kindly read it out loud. The article was about a recent poll stating that 51% of every man and woman in the country was planning to read the last book in the world. *Rrrread*. She rolled on the r and snorted, as if she couldn't believe what the world had come to. I didn't take it personal, I never did when it came to Mrs. Hardgrave, but there was something about her comment that struck a chord. Suddenly it dawned on me; in order to coax the language of greatness out of whatever distant land it resided in, I had to reread them. I had to reread every single book.

Weeks passed. I spent most of the time on the mattress, reading book after book. Every now and then I called Mr. Krista, who by now was quite used to my phone calls, and regardless of my requests, always ended our conversations with the same "anything else you need, don't hesitate to call." It went so far I was thinking of requesting something extraordinary, like an elephant, just to see what he'd say. But I never did.

By the time the pile of reread books towered over me, I had lost count of exactly how much time had passed. With the words of a thousand sentences swirling around in my head, I walked over to the window to look outside. I was surprised to see a pallid funnel moving across the street – the wind had picked up a mass of discarded plastic wrappings, busying itself by spinning them around, before it suddenly stopped and the trash again lay dead and unmoving on the ground. I scratched the beard that covered my face, and had the decelerating world outside not told me, I wouldn't have known. It was already fall.

I'd been so cooped up in my house on the mountain, everything I needed supplied at the push of a button, that the season had changed without me. I started up my computer and stared at the numbers in the upper-right corner. I'd been holed up for almost two months to the day!

I made a quick dash around the room to get a grip on things. I counted the books in the pile next to my mattress – I'd managed nearly one a day, a feat on its own, but so far the effort had yielded nothing. I had written but a page here and there, and then only about the anguish of not knowing what to write. I could feel the jaws of failure opening around me.

Eventually I calmed down. I shaved, purging myself of anxiety, and once I felt clean, cleansed even, things no longer seemed all that bad. There was still plenty of time, and, I argued with myself, wasn't really most of writing done in not-writing anyway? The collecting of thoughts, the devouring of inspiration? The writing was merely the mechanics that followed the blueprint the mind had already dreamt up.

So I settled back into my rhythm and tried to forget all about it. I said to myself, *An artist knows not, and cares not, about the shackles of time.* Stress and pressure were two ingredients that I had to keep away from the pot at all costs, and I began my exercise by picking up a new book from the unread pile.

Meanwhile the autumn storms raged outside, but the tearing winds didn't concern me. On the contrary, I quite enjoyed the soft sound of their fruitless attempts to thump their way into the century-old structure, hurting no one but themselves. What they did manage, however, was to lower the temperature inside, so I had a couple of sacks of firefood brought up. That was what we called it – we still do, I suppose – *firefood*, the artificial fruit of some heat-starved scientist, and then neither wind nor the changing of seasons could disturb me.

Henceforth my evenings were lit up by a nice, inviting fire, and it was a marvel to see, the way the flames went from yellow to a dark glowing orange within the hour, and each night I fell asleep listening to the soft hissing and cracking of the coals.

I kept reading, always prepared with the notebook in case a window opened, until I was finally down to the last five. An increasing feeling of unease came over me as I began on that final pile, and it grew in size with every book I finished. Then, one day, there was only one left.

It was an especially cold and raw day, where the smoke from the chimneys in the distance was swept away as soon as it was released into the sky and waves of icy wind crashed untiringly upon the library, again and again. I piled the fireplace high and watched the flames take hold. I indulged in a mint and tried to relax. I dragged the mattress closer to the fire, so close that I was afraid that the heat would cause my pants to ignite, and only then did the clump of ice in my stomach begin to melt. And with that I picked up the remaining book and started reading.

6

Days pass. I lie in my hospital bed at night and walk the streets to the bakery in the morning to check on the fire, but other than that nothing much occurs. At times I consider accepting the fact that I may still be dreaming, that I am still on my mattress in front of the fireplace. I feel years away from falling asleep there, and if that were the case, there are a few details that worry me: my head, for one, it's healing fine. And how would it be possible for me to fall asleep every night and wake every morning, and still be in the same dream? Today I even tried to force myself past the wall of heat to see if it would be enough to finally rouse me from my hibernation, but all I managed to do was burn the tip of my ears.

Instead I decide to try another idea: I'll find Hemingway. If I am truly here, in *A Farewell to Arms*, then Hemingway must be around somewhere. If I can somehow prove that he isn't here, or never has been, then I know I am delusional, trapped in a dream perhaps, but nothing worse.

I begin at the hospital: I ask all the nurses and doctors about him, but I draw a blank. I can't really picture him without his beard, so that's how I describe him. "Hemingway," I say, "white beard, like Santa Claus." But the nurses only laugh at me and say in broken English that the blow to my head must have been harder than they thought. I then ask the baker, but he knows of no such man, although he promises to ask his friends about him. Then it strikes me that the one place where they would know I haven't been. The soldiers' quarters.

The porter announces that the major will see me in his office. He is seated behind his desk as I step inside and I take note of the two bunks behind him. He looks old and tired with grey streaks in his hair, and he doesn't stand, nor attempt to shake my hand.

"Sit." He motions with his head toward an empty chair. "What can I do for you?"

I'm eager to make a good impression, so I lie.

"I'm a journalist with the *New Library Times*. I'm an American," I add and watch the major's face for any signs, but it is cut from stone.

"I am here reporting on the war, and I've heard there is an American ambulance driver in the area by the name of Hemingway. Ernest Hemingway."

The major seems to contemplate this, and I want to tell him about the beard and the drinking and the fishing trips in the Keys, the bullfighting and the women, when suddenly he interrupts.

"No, signor, sorry." And with that he turns his attention back to his desk and his typewriter, with the efficient signature military stiffness.

The rest of the day passes uneventfully. I stroll around town and halfheartedly inquire about Hemingway at random, but nothing comes of it, and when I've taken my supper in bed and am again watching the bats chasing insects across the darkening evening sky, I dwell on the first scenario. What if I really am stuck in a dream?

I lie sleepless in the darkness. For a few hours it is complete and total, outside is inside and vice versa, the walls are sky, the windows removed, and everything in the room, including the bed, has melted into blackness; it's as if I am floating in an underwater cave. A dream is a parody of life...or was it the other way around? I try to remember what the great ones said, and as I retrace words and stories and important ideas in my head, I come to think of the list. *The list.* I get out of bed in search of my pants; moments later the list is in my hand. *A Handful of Dust* by Evelyn Waugh. I turn the lights out and try to remember it, then more vividly, and more, and more, until I fall asleep inside the realm of *The Waste Land.*

When I open my eyes I am at Brat's, the gentlemen's club where young men can be merry without the muttering from older members. For a few moments I blink my eyes to remove the dust, but still the room and everything in it seems to be in a simmer or a slight haze, the dreamy mist refusing to clear. I am in a leather Morris chair, a rather peculiar one that is reclining back so violently it is almost spilling my body onto the floor. Because of the steep angle, when I look towards the bar across the room, I have to tuck my chin to my chest.

The bar is lined with wide, suit-coated backs. They stand shoulder to shoulder along the entire length, as if protecting it from any intruder who dared attempt to break through. The men are all young – well, younger than the old – and by the way the great backs twitch and shake every now and then, I know they are jolly. From out of nowhere, a man suddenly sits down next to me.

"Evening, old boy."

He was, no doubt, once considered distinguished in that old-fashioned snobby British way, but now, for some reason, his hair is a mess of frizzled hanks, his skin so oily and red that one would expect it to shortly dry and fall off in great big flakes. Around his eyes dark hollows creep. Before I can think of a proper greeting, he continues.

"You are the first one I speak to for days. Dr. Messinger left in the canoe, and he told me to stay put, so here I am. But the bicyclists, they keep going by. They make me very tired."

I have a hard time understanding anything of what the man says, but I don't want to be rude. "That sounds like hard cheese."

"What? Oh, yes, hard cheese. But don't give any to the mechanical mouse. It really did scare Brenda, you see, and now she's gone and put up that chromium plating. Thinks it will protect her, poor thing."

A barman, looking very smart in his stiff white shirt, black vest, and shiny hair, appears and puts two glasses on the table between us.

"I am Mr. Last," the man says and picks up his glass in a salute.

"I am Butter, Jonathan Butter," I say and likewise raise mine. Mr. Last sips his drink and scrunches up his face.

"Nasty medicine, this." He says, his eyes overflowing with tears. For a moment we say not another word, and then he begins to sob.

"What's wrong?" I say, for I feel I ought to at least ask.

"It's the horse. That and Mr. Beaver. He took the horse away at night, and now it is in Belgravia for three guineas a week. It studies economics, but Ben says it should keep its bloody legs shut."

I catch her by a stroke of the eye; a woman with a great big hat on her head walks in by the bar, scanning it for something or someone.

"It would be more polite if you listened when I addressed you instead of biking back and forth like that. It makes my head spin, and I can't say I have much of a patience with child's games."

Finally, the woman seems to have found who she was searching for and walks straight over to where Mr. Last and I are sitting.

"Tony!" she exclaims in a feigned surprise, opening her arms and bending forward for a proper hello. When she does I notice the tail dragging over the floor from under her dress.

"Polly, how lovely. You aren't afraid of mechanical mice, are you?"

The tail is grey and covered in fur, and it rolls up and unrolls with lively movement as she talks to Mr. Last. I can't take my eyes off it; only when she quiets do I look up and see that her hat is really a cock's skinny beard standing straight out from her neck.

"Mr. Beaver," Polly says curtly and nods my way. I look over both my shoulders but can't spot anyone. *Perhaps she is just as crazy as Mr. Last,* I think.

A sudden bout of applause turns my attention toward the bar. A horse has entered, and on it a boy, no more than eleven years old, sits crouching forward, leaning against the horse's wide neck so as not to hit his head on a roof beam.

"You must come visit Hetton," Mr. Last says, adding in a convincing voice, "We shall pick flowers and maybe even play us a game of Animal Snap." Polly coughs into the powder case she holds open, and a cloud of pink escapes from it. The horse lets out a gnawing neigh – the men at the bar are still standing with their backs towards it, only turning their necks – then jerks back and in a sudden movement rears up, waving two front legs like scissors through the air. The boy slams first into the roof beam, then bounces from it onto the floor, where he lies motionless in a small pile.

"You must come," Mr. Last says, "but let's not bicycle. I'm too tired for bicycling, and Mr. Messinger told me to stay put."

Polly lets out a startled shriek; then, swinging from chandelier to chandelier, she chatters and shows her teeth while whisking her tail through the air.

"I shall even read to you," Mr. Last says, and everywhere I look in the room, at the boy lying under the horse, the wide backs at the bar, the man incoherently babbling beside me, and Polly chattering from the middle of the room, there's a pink layer of dust covering everything.

I open my eyes and I notice at once how warm and sticky my body feels. It's past dawn, but not much, and I don't know what it means that I see the room from my hospital bed, or the trees outside the windows, not until I see the list resting on my stomach. I lie within myself, very still, trying to keep the panic at bay, to not let it even know I am awake.

It works; after a while, the threat has passed and I know exactly where I am. I know without looking that there's a tray on the floor beside the bed, I know that the bakery opens soon, I know that the major, with his stern face and efficient manners, is probably already sitting at his desk, and I know that the bandage on my head is coming off today. What was it then? A dream? A dream within a dream of a dream? I dare not even begin to understand.

After lunch the nurse unwinds the gauze from my head. I'm in bed, waiting for the doctor, and when he arrives twenty minutes later the major is with him. They seem to be arguing. While the doctor proceeds to examine my head, the major speaks.

"The man you look for – I shouldn't be telling you this – but there is another ambulance driver, an American. Tenente Henry. Tenente Frederic Henry." Too much at once is happening around my head, with the doctor leaning in, looking closely at my scalp and pressing his delicate fingers into my temples.

"Hemingway?" I say and glance at the major from under the doctor's hands.

"No, Tenente Henry," the major says and winks his eye at me.

I find it very peculiar, the wink, but I nod slowly. The major tightens up and straightens out, flashes me a gentleman's salute, and leaves the room. The doctor follows soon after, giving me two thumbs-up. It's all very peculiar, and then the information makes its impact. *Tenente* means "lieutenant" in Italian. Hemingway was obviously never Hemingway in his books! Frederic Henry, the American ambulance driver in love with Catherine Barkley. With a slurry of ice around my spine, I hear a jingle and I know it is the keys to my prison.

Days come and go, and when I sleep I dream, and when I wake up I am still here. That leaves me with only one viable explanation; the spell placed on me by that sinister character Koob, is real. In other words, I'm truly and utterly screwed.

Is this it, then? Is this the end of the line? What if I get on a ship and cross the ocean? Would I arrive back in the future? Would the world disintegrate and fall to pieces? Everything here feels so real: the cobblestones, the water in the fountain, the scabs on my head. What if I die here? Will my body draw its last breath on the floor in the library? Is it only my mind that has been hijacked? I have so many questions, but no answers. This is a hell of a thing I've gotten myself into, a hell of a thing.

7

I remember when I knew it was all over. The night before, through the sphere of light cast from a streetlight just outside, I saw snowflakes fall. The books were all ploughed through, savagely violated, their protective cardboard gutted. They lay in disorderly piles on the floor next to the mattress, with some piles so high they blocked my view of the fireplace completely. Only above the lower heaps did I see the flames dance, like fires in the remains of some bombed-out city.

All I could do was call my own bluff. My mind was not in the order I had expected it to be, and my ideas for writing were, if possible, even further from the surface than when I began. I was very disappointed. With hindsight I wonder if the trick to greatness really isn't to stay away from it all. To not meddle with the purity. Then ideas will be new, not inbred offspring impregnated time and again. That night, every thought I had, every sentence I formed in my head, was a fragment of other peoples' sentences and thoughts. If it's true that a man is the sum of his thoughts, then by reading those hundred books I had indubitably lost myself.

I'm not sure where it came from, the tremendous rage. A deep and burning anger suddenly scorched my insides, and the only thing I knew for sure, the only thing that glowed with the clarity of fact, was that I hated the books around me. They were to blame for everything that had happened, I reasoned, and in a momentary outrage my hand reached out, grabbed a book from the nearest pile, and hurled it right into the fire.

For a brief moment the flames were disrupted, seemingly unsure of what had so suddenly imposed on them. The force of impact had sent a cloud of tiny glowing nettles into the air, and as they slowly floated back towards the fire, the flames at last recognized the intruder as food and pounced on it. In the bat of an eyelash, the book exploded in a blazing inferno.

But my anger was far from quelled. My hand reached out again, and again, graciously halting to wait for the small explosion before it continued. It was curious how it seemed time itself stood still, my anger so great it was as if the fire I was feeding raged also inside of me. Only when I was down to a stack of the last ten books did I at last feel soothed, my senses calmed. In fact, I was drained of all energy, and for no other reason than to finish what I had started, I fed the last ten books to the fire before I fell like a log onto the mattress.

When I regained my consciousness the fireplace was dark and cold. I looked around the room, rubbing the sleep from my eyes, and I wondered for a brief moment where all the books had gone. My brothers in arms, my guiding stars. Only too soon did I remember. Rolling across my mattress towards the charred opening, I discovered that all that remained of the world's hundred greatest novels was the corner of a cover that had somehow managed to escape the fire's endless hunger. I put my finger on the burned cardboard and solemnly dragged it from the ashes. I felt a great shame fill my entire chest – it was sad to see a book this way, a symbol of freedom broken and disfigured – and I flipped it back into the fireplace.

A harsh, steely light seeped in through the window; I had a feeling that if I got up and looked outside I'd discover that everything was covered in a thick, white layer of snow. It was a depressing thought, and I braced myself for it, when suddenly the world was snapped into pitch darkness.

Something had entered my lungs, and I was coughing wildly. I hacked and gasped for air, and through the dark I could hear the echoes of my own guttural moans bounce back from the inner sanctuary of the fireplace. It took several long seconds of blind confusion before I managed to wipe my eyes clear with the bottom of my shirt.

Teary-eyed, I slowly watched a picture of the room develop. I coughed again and swallowed hard a couple of times, spitting out a gob of black soot. It landed on the floor in front of me with a sinister splatter. It was while examining it that my ears alerted me to a conflict of perception; something didn't measure up. Even though my mouth was closed, the coughing persisted.

It was a deep hacking whoop, dark and muffled, and it was coming from inside the fireplace. For every cough a small plume of black shot out into the room, and my mind conjured up a picture of a pigeon, or a raccoon, stuck inside the chimney, clawing at the walls in panic. I dropped to my knees, to one side of the tenebrous clouds, and carefully leaned forward to see if I couldn't spot the poor creature. So determined was I to find it that even when I heard the voice, an animal was all I could picture.

"I beg your pardon. It's been quite some time," the voice said between coughs, and I had to duck under yet another billow of smoke.

I was flabbergasted. I leant forward and looked up the black hole. *Surely a person couldn't fit in there,* I told myself, but, with no regard to my opinion, the voice continued.

"It was that last piece that did it."

The voice came from so close by it was as if it was speaking right into my ear. Again I felt it stir in the pit of my stomach – anger – but this time I tried to control it. I got up so I could better examine the dark opening, to locate the hidden speakers. At the time I was convinced there was a camera in the room. In my mind it suddenly made perfect sense that they'd want to keep an eye on their golden goose.

I scrambled back and forth, patting the chimney with my hands, all while the coughing sounds were replaced by a weird humming that soon filled the entire room. But no matter how I searched I couldn't find anything attached to the rough finish of the fireplace, or anywhere in the ceiling or along the floor. After a while the steady humming had turned into a constant drone, an ongoing tone without highs or lows, and it annoyed me to such a degree that finally my anger got the best of me. I leant into the fireplace and hollered up the chimney.

"Hey!!!"

It worked. The humming stopped, but before I knew what hit the world was again snapped into darkness. I stumbled to the back of the room, as far away as possible from the fireplace, and again I had to use my shirt to clear my stinging eyes. This time the voice returned even before the world became visible.

"Pardon my behavior, but I have slept all too long in the very depths of silence to be able to stand this shouting right in my ear."

"Woo...who...what...what? " I stuttered, attempting to focus in the direction of the voice.

"Who are you?"

"Why, pardon me again. I'm afraid also my manners have been asleep far too long. I am Koob, delightfully at your service."

The room finally emerged from behind the drapes of mist, and what I saw bewildered me even more than the voice itself. Staring back at me from across the room, so help me God, was a giant face. What were before two windows were now rectangular eyes, and what was up until this fateful morning a fireplace had turned into a gaping mouth. The edge of the mantelpiece was bending with the shape and smoothness of a soft lip, with every breath moving a small puff of black smoke in and out of the vivid darkness. As surely as my name is Jonathan Butter, the fireplace had become one large and very real mouth.

"Koob?" I said, not intending to pose a question.

"Yes, sir?"

As the monstrous mouth formed the words the windows – I mean the eyes focused attentively on me, as if waiting for me to speak.

"I...I must be dreaming..." was all I managed to get out.

"Not at all, my dear boy, not at all. I can assure you that this is all very real. You woke me, and now here I am, at your service."

"W...woke you?"

"Yes, and I am forever grateful for it. I can't even begin to tell you how lonely an eternal sleep can get. Time is without borders in that faraway place. You should have seen..."

"Stop!" As uneasy as it made me feel, I directed my shout towards the fireplace, and at once the room fell silent. I welcomed the familiar absence of sound, and let it sit there for a while before I continued.

"Are you saying," I began, hardly believing the words that came out of my own mouth, "that you are some sort of a genie, but instead of in a bottle, you've been trapped in a library fireplace? And now – wait, don't tell me – now I get to make a wish? And anything I wish for will be granted me?"

"Except that you can't ask for another wish, yes," the voice replied cordially.

I felt my legs turn into jelly and disappear under me. Leaning against the wall, I slithered down, inch by inch – I had turned into one of those slimy toys – all the way to the floor. I let my head fall forward into my hands and, encapsulated this way from the outside world, I made the silence my one and only focus. *I must still be sleeping,* I told myself, but when I opened my eyes, the face across the room was still looking at me like a dog at his master.

"I am the demon of books, the protector of imagination and dreams caught within the boundary of paper – except in the last few decades, when I haven't been able to protect much of anything. It was the burning of books that placed me in these chains. It was a vile time, and I shall not go into it further, but as nature has it, the yin and the yang, the death within life, and so on, it was the return of the fire, your little demonstration last night, that finally unlocked the door to my prison. And for that freedom I am eternally grateful."

The mouth stopped moving and I stared at it across the room. It was a ridiculous story if I had ever heard one, a demon locked inside a fireplace? Correction, a *demon of books* locked inside a fireplace.

"I ask you again, is there anything I can do for you?"

The voice from the fireplace rang friendly through the room, but I couldn't take it seriously. Only really as a response to my own thoughts, as one would speak above the head of a child too young to understand, did I exhale and say, "I wish only for one thing, and that is to finish my book."

"Very well then," the voice replied cheerfully. "Tomorrow is a new day. Now, if you will excuse me." And with that the blinds suddenly spilled down from top of the windows with a hurried razzle, shutting both eyes, and when I next looked at the gaping darkness it had transformed back to being just an ordinary fireplace.

There I sat in the ensuing silence, completely stupefied, unable to move or think.

"It was only a dream," I mumbled, and finally I reclined onto on the mattress and closed my eyes.

I was right, it really was snow. I woke up early, and the first thing I did was look out the window. The entire city lay beneath an icing of cool white, and every angle that was just a few days ago quadrant and sharp was now soft and smooth. I recalled the dream from last night in great detail as I looked at the white-capped landscape and wondered what could have brought on a vision so vivid, when suddenly the landscape disappeared and I was staring straight into a great rectangular eye.

"Good morning, Jonathan," the voice said, and once again, I took a leap backwards.

"You really need to find another way of waking me up. Throwing pieces of cardboard down my throat and poking me in the eye early in the morning isn't very pleasant."

Before I had a chance to even compute what the voice was saying, it continued.

"So, Jonathan, are you ready?"

"Ready?" I repeated. "Ready for what?"

"Why, to begin your book of course."

What was happening to me? I couldn't understand it, yet I didn't turn and run. I didn't scream or even stomp my foot on the floor. I just stood there, like a rabbit caught in the headlights.

"Come stand closer," the voice coaxed me. "Right here in front of me. Now close your eyes and relax."

The voice was strangely soothing, almost hypnotizing, and as if under some sort of spell I did as I was told. There was a light draft along the floor; I figured the windows had opened, but I kept my eyes shut. For every second that passed the draft increased, and soon it had grown so powerful that I felt my pant legs flapping in the wind.

"Keep your eyes closed, Jonathan," the voice urged, but when the suction increased so much I began to wobble, instinctively I peeked through a slit in my eyes. Just as I did, a mighty gust lifted me up and swept me from where I stood, catapulting me into the fireplace, and the last image on my retina before the world went black was the upside-down view of the room in which I'd spent the last months.

8

Time passes quickly, yet it's peculiar how it doesn't move at all. My head is now completely healed and since my inquiries about Tenente Henry has led nowhere, I have reverted into a tedious routine that consists of going for walks around town and reading an old English Bible in my room. I find it rather strange that the hospital hasn't asked me to leave – I get my trays of food just like I always have, but there's never a word about my stay here. So while I'm well fed and cared for, I'm beginning to feel bored out of my mind. There's only so much walking and reading the words of God a man can do.

I try to keep my sanity intact, and as I often do in the evenings I sit under the mulberry tree just outside the hospital, brooding over my choices. The sun has already disappeared behind the mountains, and night is fast approaching, when I notice a peculiar man crossing the square. He emerges from the south corner and walks swiftly towards the north side. He doesn't notice me where I sit because I'm very still, and the mulberry tree casts a shadow so large it covers me completely. What's peculiar about the man is not the way he walks, or the fact that he anxiously looks over his shoulder, but the clothes he is wearing. He is dressed for leisure, by the time's standards, in beige chinos, a blue shirt with the top three buttons undone, and a chic red scarf tied around his neck. And I wouldn't have thought twice about it, had it not been for his shoes. At first I don't notice them, but there's something about the way he is crossing the square, and just when he passes outside the shadow of the tree, I happen to catch it. It's the lack of sound. And that's when I notice his sneakers.

I let him pass to the other side of the square before I get up to follow. I could have sworn those were modern sneakers – more modern than any appearing in a Hemingway novel should be, anyway.

The man continues to advance in the same careful manner, with me never closer than thirty steps behind, until we emerge from the narrow streets and come upon an opening where the river flows along several feet below us. I lose sight of him for a moment – it's only a matter of seconds, but enough for my heart to go wild. I can't afford to let my only clue go astray, and I scramble in the dusky light. Finally I spot him on the other side of the bridge, a different shade of pale in the surrounding pallidity, just about to climb down onto the riverbank.

They're not even real steps, just a series of jagged rocks protruding from the wall, and for a second after I drop the last bit onto the thick sand I dare not move. I listen while I try to spy through the darkness cast by the bridge. The river is pouring by with gentle perseverance, creating only the slightest babble with its unbending flow, but the man is nowhere to be seen. I continue all the way in under the arch and take a seat on a single rock half buried in the sand. *Perhaps he spotted me and went up the other side of the bridge,* I think just before I see the door.

Immediately inside, a long corridor stretches out, cut straight through the stone as it seems. Its damp, dark walls are illuminated by lightbulbs that cast a steady glow every five steps, but there's no seeing the end of it. I swallow hard and with one last glance at the mercury-smooth river, I step forward and let the door to who-knows-what, close behind me.

The jagged walls feel slippery under my hand, and I pussy-foot forward. *If something goes wrong, I can be out by the river again in no time,* I tell myself as I stop in front of yet another door. I wrap my fingers around the handle, and I give myself a few good pats on the back. *This is just a dream,* I repeat in my mind, even though I now know that is far from true.

The stairs behind the door lead only one way, and maybe it's my imagination, but I think I hear the soft echo of footsteps trailing off way above; it must be the man with the sneakers.

The metal-grid structure and see-through landings trembles and shakes as I climb, and when I reach the top I continue through a new corridor, much like the one I just left behind, although not quite as damp, until I reach another door. Perhaps I've become too comfortable too quickly, and for the first time since the square am I careless.

By the mighty pyramids of Egypt! The world is emptied upon me all at once. The light, the sound, the green leaves of the trees; I step outside and *shazaam*! I am on a sidewalk facing a park, and behind me, across a street where colorful cars zoom by, tall buildings reach for the sky. All around me there's loud honking, the razzle of bike chains, tires licking asphalt, and a steady humming that makes the air vibrate. I stagger away from the door, the shift so sudden that it takes twice the neuron synapses for my mind to comprehend; I can hear it bubbling as they rush towards the message center between my ears, and through the auditory and visual chaos my eyes automatically attach themselves to something familiar. I spot him just as he walks into a building across the street, the man in the red scarf and sneakers. *The Once Upon a Time Palace Café* reads the sign above the entrance in black lacquered letters that give the impression of lighting up at night. I am stunned, but I keep staggering forward. I cross the street and duly take note that I, in some as-yet inconceivable way, have been transported to New York City.

Perhaps the corridors are the connective tissue between dream and reality, I think as I reach the entrance and put my hands on the two golden bars bent in the smooth shape of a U.

The doors of the Once Upon a Time Palace Café are heavy and open up majestically to each side. They seem to have been hacked out of one single, gigantic tree trunk, the two pieces similarly dark and smooth, carrying with them a slight scent of cinnamon. I have to lean back with my full body weight to shake them from a standstill, and yet they close behind me with an astounding lack of sound.

I think I must have made a mistake. I expect to find myself in a café – per the sign outside – but I must have opened the wrong doors. The plush red carpet under my feet, the heavy moss green drapes and the rich wood panels that cover the walls, makes it look more like a posh private club than a café. There's nobody's around, the maître d's podium stands empty, and I tread forward, the carpet swallowing up every little sound my feet make. At the very end of the lobby, across an intersection where a corridor carries the plush carpet both left and right, there is another door. On the wall right next to it I notice a small brass plaque that reads *Milk Bar.* I run my hand gently over the door; it gives way, swaying loosely back and forth on silent hinges, and I push through, at last finding myself in the café.

Suddenly the penny falls through the slot: blood rushes from my head and makes the entire room spin. I reach a stool just in time and, breathing deep, I focus hard on an imaginary diamond that sits nestled right between my eyebrows. *None of this is real, none of this is real,* I repeat, over and over again.

When my lightheadedness has cleared I look up and see that I'm on one of a line of stools running along the bar. Identical round, red-leather seats stick up from the floor like buttons. It's an old fifties place, with pastel tiles on the wall behind the counter and, above it, a mirror that reflects not only the soda jerk in his milk-white apron and hat, but also a gaggle of milkshake mixers, myself, and, behind me, a jukebox with a bright yellow neon rim. It makes me feel like a character in a Hopper painting. I gaze through the mirror at the entire room, at the tables where people sit with tall glasses topped with whipped cream and red cherries, at the hamburgers with so many layers it seems a mean feat that they even stay upright, and at the picture of Babe Ruth on the wall. I'm taking it all in, when a voice next to me pulls me out of the reflection.

"They have very nice milkshakes here, indeed."

On the stool next to mine, well-nigh too short to reach the counter, sits a little boy. His hair is straw-yellow, and around his shoulders hangs a cloak of a richness worn by kings, purple on the inside and a bright blue on the outside.

"Quite nice, especially the strawberry cream," the boy continues, and dangling from his side, as he kicks his legs back and forth, is a wooden sword.

"It's my first time here," I say and continue to study him.

He is a clever boy – I can tell by the way he squints, a serious expression across his face, as many thoughts about everything roll about inside his pint-sized head.

"Well, then, a very great welcome to you."

After a moment of silence, still kicking his legs, he says, "Take my word for it. You must try the milkshakes."

It suddenly strikes me just why he is going on about the milkshakes.

"Would you like one?"

"Thank you, but you needn't buy me one. Everything is free here. Haven't they told you? It's all part of the deal."

"The deal?" I say.

"Yes, the deal" the boy repeats.

"I see," I say, although I really have no idea what he is talking about. It occurs to me is that he seems awfully young to be at a café all by himself.

"What's your name? Are you here alone?" I ask.

"Oh, you have to guess."

"Guess what your name is or if you are here alone?"

"Both. Draw me a sheep."

"Excuse me?"

"Draw me a sheep."

"I don't understand. Where are your parents?"

"Because where I live everything is so small? The boa that ate the elephant that looked like a hat? The sheep inside the box?"

"I'm afraid I don't follow. Do your parents work here?"

"Okay, listen closely and I'll tell you, but only because you are new. Are you ready?"

"Mmm." I say, looking around the room.

"The asteroid where I am from is called B-612. A Turkish astronomer first observed it in 1909, but because his clothes were funny no adults believed him. Easy, right?"

"I think we ought to…"

"The baobabs? They start out small and grow and grow and grow and eventually threaten to overtake the entire planet. I say it's really a question of discipline, and that's very true. And there's also a tame fox."

It's the mention of the baobabs. It rips open a small hole where the first trickle of recognition seeps through, before it bursts open and the revelation lands on me with a splash.

"Aha! So, you are…?"

"Yes, I am."

"But…we are not in the desert. This is an ice cream parlor."

The little prince breaks out in a lovely peal of laughter, shaking his head as if this was the funniest thing he ever did hear.

"You are funny," he says and turns to face the mirror. "Now how about that milkshake?"

"Just wait a minute," I say, now quite annoyed, feeling as if this whole disturbing set of dreams, or whatever my mind wants to call them, has gone one step too far.

"Where did you say we are? What is this place if not another dream?"

"Ha-ha, you really are funny! You remind me of the airman. In the beginning he is also very, hmm… what's the word, skeptical? Yes, he is skeptical and only wants to work on his aeroplane engine, and now you are acting the same way."

"Can you please just tell me if this is a dream or not!" My voice manages to hide none of my annoyance.

"Hold on," the boy says and turns to face me.

It is an intelligent face that looks up at mine, young and innocent, yet filled with years of experience. Like a child actor born into the theater, so very used to stage that the edges between acting and life itself have been erased.

"You don't belong here."

He says it to himself, punctuating a thought.

"You are not from around here, are you? I've heard of you – well, not of you personally, but your kind. I have just never met one before."

"One what?"

"A visitor," the prince answers with a sigh, as if *I* hadn't listened to a word he said.

With this I feel myself breaking down. I mean, I actually feel parts of my body break off and fall to the floor. I don't want to be locked in my head anymore. I can't talk to apparitions and figures of my own imagination, keep a straight face and go along with the ride in the hopes of waking up. I feel the loneliest I have ever felt in my entire life, betrayed by my own mind, the one thing I thought I could always trust. I just want to go home. I ignore the prince and everyone else in the room – they are not real. Yet when I feel the tears coming, I bury my head in my arms.

Everything in there is dark and muffled, but I can still hear the prince speaking in the background. Oh, how did I ever get into this mess! Was it the pressure of winning the competition? Did Mr. Krista drug me? If I could just focus intensely on who I am, where I am from, I should be able to break free from the grips of my mind. I press my thoughts in what I think is the right direction, I squeeze them through a needle's eye of the little reality I have left, but I lose it all when I feel a tiny hand on my shoulder. I hear the prince's encouraging words ring through my left ear.

"Try the milkshake, it really is good."

When I open my eyes, two glasses are standing on the counter in front of us. They are filled to the brim, actually well above the brim, with creamy, white froth, and through the glass, all the way down the side, which is wet with condensation, tiny bits of red shine through. I'm guessing they are strawberries.

"Try it," the prince eggs me on, still the little boy in a costume, yet with such command. "I promise you'll feel better."

I haven't really noticed before – I only realize as I stick my lips into the froth – but I do feel awfully hungry.

"Mmmm, this is delicious," I manage to get out before I dive into it again.

"I told you so," the prince says, and smiles.

I slurp up more than half the contents before I have to pause to take another breath. I sit back to let the cool cream settle in my stomach, while the boy explains.

"This isn't really how it's done. I mean, I don't think I'm even allowed to tell you this – we're supposed to uphold the story to the outside at all times. Except I've never met a visitor before, and well, I sort of feel sorry for you. By the way, did you know that most visitors end up in hospitals? The loony bin. At least, that's what I've heard. You see, in reality, outside of the covers, nobody really believes them. Except for other visitors. But what good is a loon to another loon, right?"

I feel like I am back with Koob in the library that first morning, with an abnormality revealing itself in front of my eyes. Only this time I don't let the surprise catch me off guard.

"Where am I?"

"Well, this is the Once Upon a Time Palace Café, but we simply call it the Palace. It's a pretty big place, hence the palace part. I don't think I've even been to all the rooms."

"But... what is this place?"

"Well, you see..." The prince searches for something in my face.

"Jonathan. Jonathan Butter."

"Well, you see, Jonathan, first of all, this is not a dream."

I look at the prince, the boy who is supposedly the little prince, and I can't even remember all the steps I've taken to get here. He sees my disbelief and continues before I can protest.

"Simply put, this is where we take a rest from performing. I suppose you could call it our dressing room."

"Your dressing room?"

"You have to understand, some of us have been performing for well over a hundred years – you never know just how long you'll be called up for. It can be every day for a very long time, or there is just an endless wait. You'll see the latter, eventually, in the Bar of Once Upon."

"But... what are you? And what's out there?" I say and nod towards the street.

"You really are lost, aren't you?" the prince says and takes a swig from his milkshake. "Out there is nothing. It's sort of like a lobby to this place. It's only the one block, like one of those glass bubbles filled with water. You shake it and watch the snowflakes fall, but it only really happens inside the bubble. The Palace is where we all come in between jobs. Our real homes are within the covers."

"I still don't get it," I say.

I watch the little prince, the white line the shape of a half-moon where the far end of the glass touched between his eyes, but I can't believe the words that come out of his mouth.

"We are characters," he says, and the half-moon bends as he raises his eyebrows. "And this is our café."

The little prince excuses himself – he says he is due back for another round. I watch him adjust his cape so it sits just right, wipe his face clean, cross the room and disappear through the entrance. I think about what I've just been told. A café filled with characters? Characters on a break from performing? I let the last mouthful of delicious milkshake glide down my throat before I get up.

Outside I notice the hut across the street out of which I first arrived. It looks like some sort of subway service entrance, but I ignore it for now and turn the corner. It's New York all right. Central Park is alive behind my back while I'm walking south – to my left is the Palace, a colossus made of brick and stone, stretching in one solid piece all the way down to the next intersection. I'm not sure exactly where I'm heading, and when I am about to cross the street over to the next block down, exactly halfway over, something incredible happens: I am stopped short.

By that I mean that when I get to the middle of the street I suddenly can't go any further – an invisible wall is blocking my way. I run my hands over it: it's smooth – not like glass, not like anything I've ever felt – and it extends in all directions. I move to the left, and there it is. I jump up, and there it is, the same smooth surface. I bend down and feel it coming out of the asphalt, solid but invisible. I begin treading east and the invisible wall is there with me, down the middle of the street, until I hit the corner the next block over. There is another sudden stop where the wall changes direction and extends north. Behind it everything looks the same, a sort of glass bubble reality, with people and cars coming and going, only nobody seems to take notice of the wall. And what's worse, nobody takes notice of me. I bang on the wall as hard as I can, but it doesn't budge one bit, and my screams might as well have been screams trapped inside a jar, because nobody bats an eye in my direction. All that comes from it is the sound of the meaty slapping from my own palms.

On my way back into the Palace someone passes me and slips out through the gigantic doors just before they shut. In the corner of my eye I notice it's the man in the red scarf.

"Whoa, hey! Wait!" I say and hurry to catch him.

"Hey, baby, careful with the shirt. They only give me one."

"Signor Tenente," I say, my mind working one step ahead.

"Yeah baby?"

"I...," I begin, but suddenly I don't know what to say.

"Do we know each other?"

"Well yes, and no. I'm a friend of Mr. Henry's," I add.

"Ah, yes. We work together for a long time now. I am Rinaldi."

"Nice to meet you," I say.

There's silence between us.

"I must go," Rinaldi says. "Have to get back to duty."

"Please Sir, can I ask you something?" I must sound desperate, for Rinaldi steps closer and puts his hand on my arm.

"It's just that...well, I am very new here and don't know my way around. I need to find Koob," I say.

"Koob?"

"Yes, in the fireplace."

"Ah, the fireplace. This is easy. You go straight until you see the elevator. Then go to the sixth floor, and in the first room on your left, there is the fireplace."

He leaves me there, on the sidewalk, and I watch the man called Rinaldi cross the street and disappear into the subway service entrance.

The elevator is so quiet and stable I can hardly feel it move. I concentrate on the circles above the door – I watch them light up and darken – and when the doors open the lights are the only indication we've been moving at all. The sixth floor lobby looks much the same as the first, clad with identical dark, almost reddish wood panels, and heavy green velvet drapes on the walls. It's really only the color carpet that's different – up here it's dark blue, a real plush thing, deep as a forest, and it stretches down the corridor in both directions. I hang a left and, just like Rinaldi said, I come across a door. *Smoking Room,* reads the polished brass sign.

The Smoking Room is a British hunting lodge–style lounge with stuffed heads of moose and various other trophies protruding from the walls. It reminds me a little bit of my dream of Brat's, except warmer and cozier. Below the animal trophies the walls are covered with bookshelves, and in front of them, red leather lounge chairs stand in pairs. I spot the fire at once and take a seat right in front of it. I edge up so close I can feel the heat become a hot drape on my legs.

It's a nice fire; sizable and lively, and without being wild or imposing it's burning with just enough luster. I shake my head to the waiter, who smiles and performs an almost unnoticeable bow before leaving. With determination I turn to the flames.

"Koob," I whisper, "are you there?"

Although the opening where the flames billow and the chimney that passes up the wall to be swallowed into the roof look like the mouth and the nose of some apocalyptic beast, it is not alive in any real sense. I give it a few fruitless minutes before I sit back with a sigh and let the fire be just a fire.

I've changed my mind and turn to get the waiter's attention. He comes over, swift and soundless, taking my order with a simple nod.

The glass sits on the table next to my chair, a solid, low-cut tumbler with a generous finger of whisky. In the amber liquid float three large, perfectly square ice cubes, and little by little, as I watch, alternately, the fire, the whisky, and the books on the shelves along the wall, the heat melts the ice and the amber lightens. When the ice is completely gone I reach for the glass and gulp it all down.

I don't have to wait long. It begins on my tongue, a burning that travels down my throat, where the liquid somehow ignites, and by the time it reaches the stomach my entire chest, from my navel to my Adam's apple, is an inferno. I let it sit there. I simply notice it, and without another thought I look around the room.

On the wall two antelope heads sit mounted on dark wooden plaques. They are beautiful creatures, innocent, with black, glossy, eyes and I follow the pointy snouts out to the nose, carefully comparing each to the other. I trace every whisker and move on to the white triangular patch on each cheek – I scrutinize every part of the antelope heads without finding so much as a hair differing, and the closer I look, the more it upsets me. *There can't be two exactly alike.*

If I can only prove my point, then maybe all else that is wrong with the world will fall back into place. I know this is the thought of a desperate fool, but I stand up and get so close to the wall that I am almost leaning against the fireplace's rugged finish, and I begin counting hairs on the four ears that end in identical pointy paintbrush tips. I dissect them as closely as I can and, first when my muscles begin to cramp, do I lower my neck. My cervical vertebrae grind.

I'm facing the bookshelf; the books, a mere inch from my eyes, look gigantic. The smell, that familiar smell of old paper and cloth, the sweat of a thousand fingerprints – my mind begins to race. *Tic-toc, tic-toc.* It summersaults, tumbles, flips and finally lands on two feet. *Eureka.* I have it.

"You bastard. Ignore this!" I say and throw a paperbound volume of *The Last of the Mohicans* into the fire.

Immediately the flames engulf the book. I hold my breath, and this time I am faster than he is; as the cloud of soot shoots out from the mouth I do a quick sidestep, and the only thing it darkens is the red leather chair.

"Ha-ha! You are a fast learner!" Koob exclaims, and finally I see the face I've been yearning for such a long time.

"Jonathan, what a pleasure to see you again."

"Sure." I mutter, not even trying to mask the bitterness in my voice. But it doesn't seem to face Koob.

"Whatever have you been up to since last?"

"Do you know that I nearly got killed?"

"Ah, yes. But that tone, no reason to be uncivilized."

"Uncivilized!" I am shouting now. "*You* locked me inside this god-awful dream, where first I was tortured and then nearly killed! I am a prisoner of my own mind, and *you* are telling *me* to be civilized!?"

"There there, Jonathan, now take…"

"You take me back! You take me back right now!"

The last words are howled at the top of my lungs as I leap through the air, towards the fire.

"No! Jonathan, NOOOOO!"

And that's the last thing I hear before the flames, and then darkness, engulf me for a third time.

I wake up in a pool of white – I am on my face, splayed out across the floor, and everything around me is lit up by the brightest of lights. My body is dragging somewhat behind – *transition is a bitch,* I think – and I wipe the spittle from the corner of my mouth as I sit up to catch my bearings.

From sky to floor, stretching out to infinity, everything is a formless white, a white without borders or even a horizon to break it off. *Heaven?*

I haven't but shook the sleep from my head before a surround-sounding voice, directionless and all-encompassing, booms forth from somewhere behind the brightness. And even though it's trying hard to sound dooming and bombastic, I can tell right away who it belongs to.

"I can hear it's you," I say with a mordant voice.

"My dear Jonathan, you are too smart for me. Simply too smart!"

The voice is coming from behind my back, but as soon as I turn around the source changes direction.

"Where am I now?"

"You are in-between. We are in stalemate, my friend. Neutral ground, temporarily suspended in time and space. The story is bookmarked."

Koob's voice moves from front to back, side to side, even from under the white floor, and as it trails off into the vast empty whiteness, I panic.

"Please, Koob, can't I just go back now? Back to the library?" I say desperately.

"I'm afraid that's not possible," Koob says; this time his voice, although in stereo, is coming from my left.

"I warned you about the dangers of staying longer than twenty-four hours. I particularly stressed that part, and now I'm afraid the matter is out of my hands. You know, I'm not the only entity on this side of the world. There are rules even I have to abide by. You are certainly up a gum tree."

"But what should I do? I can't just stay here forever! There must be something I can do? Please, Koob!"

"There there, Jonathan, now calm down. It so happens that there *is* one thing you can do. Just thank your lucky star that Rinaldi was so reckless. Now listen to me..."

Before his voice trails off and disappears completely into the vast emptiness, Koob instructs me to just sit tight until I become tired. I stare off into the pallidity and think about what now lies before me. With a bit of luck I might just be all right. I repeat Koob's instructions in my head: find them, one by one, follow them back, stay a day, then return to the Palace. Then do it all over again. Only ninety-six more, and then I'll be free. And no more diving into fires.

9

Just like that I am back in the red leather chair. Well, *in* is an overstatement – I am slouching so far down that my calves rest flat on the floor and my head is buried deep in the crease where the backrest meets the seat. I'm unsure of how much time has passed – the glass on the table is gone and the fireplace is empty and dark, except for a small mound of ashes in one corner. I suppose it doesn't matter. Time no longer exists. Time is now a door with ninety-six locks that need to be picked.

On my way out I pass the waiter who stands dutifully by the bar.

"Excuse me," I say.

If I'm going to do this I want to be prepared, and the first thing I need to do is freshen up.

"Do you have any showers in this place?"

"Oh, why yes, sir, we do. Just take the elevator to the fourth floor and..."

The air inside the spa is filled with an acrid smell of chlorine that tickles my nose. The girl behind the counter smiles as she hands me a towel, and from the ceiling I notice arrows pointing towards the men's changing room.

"When is it you close?" I say it casually, as if I'm an old customer.

"What do you mean?" The girl gives me a puzzled frown.

"I mean, what time do you close for the day?"

"Aha, I thought I hadn't seen your face before," the girl says, her frown now smoothed into oblivion. "You are new, right?"

Her question makes me nervous. After what the little prince and Koob told me, I'm not sure I am supposed to be here.

"Ehm, yeah. I guess I am." I answer softly.

"I knew it! Where are you from?"

But the girl doesn't wait for my reply.

"You are a..." She swerves her big eyes around and upwards, searching for an answer on her forehead. "I've got it! You are a scientist, or perhaps a writer, living this life where you go through relationship after relationship, sort of unhappy, because you are struggling to write your second novel, but mostly because you are unable to get the one girl you truly love. Am I right?"

"Ehm, I have to go," I say and begin walking towards the changing room.

When I'm out of sight, beyond the curve of the hallway, I hear her calling out from the counter.

"By the way, we never close!"

The changing room is very spacious. Large wooden benches anchor each section while the walls are covered with white rectangular frames the height of a man, within which hangers function as doorless lockers. I put my shoes inside a frame, then my shirt, and finally I remove my pants and pull the paper from my pocket. One of the giant benches holds me steady while I stare at the list. How will I ever find the right person to follow? Most characters don't have particularly determined features, not the sort that transcend the leap from word to physical appearance anyway. Not like Superman. All I know is if a person is old, fat, dark, handsome, wears a moustache or a hook for a hand, but the details of a character are made up in the reader's mind. How will I be able to distinguish Rabbit Angstrom from the hordes of supporting characters, or the brothers Karamazov from any other brothers, or Mr. Biswas from any other islander? I sigh and stick the list back in my pants pocket. There's a stack of swimming trunks on a shelf by the towels, and I decide to postpone my panic until after I've tried out the water. I need to clear my mind.

Immediately as I step inside the room the warm and damp air wraps its arms around me, as though the water isn't contained merely within the pool, but fills the entire space. The pool blinds me, the way the light penetrates the frosted windows and reflect off the blue tiles. I move up to the window and look closely for any gaps, but the frosting reveals nothing of what is on the other side. *Perhaps it's a courtyard,* I think, convincing myself that in a normal world that would be most likely.

I move down the steps into the evenly temperate water – I can't even feel it against my skin – and I watch it slowly rise up my legs where it fills the spaces between each filamentous hair. Finally, when it's high up on my thighs, I take a deep breath and let myself fall into the pool. I am weightless, momentarily suspended between land and sky, and at once my senses sharpen; already the muck in my mind is disintegrating.

I don't stay under long – I bounce back up, surfacing like a snorting walrus – and with water still running off my closed eyelids, a voice booms forth from behind my back.

"Watch it, buddy!"

I see through the haze a man just passing on my left, starting up towards the far end of the pool, and I feel the smoke before I even see the cigarette. I can hardly believe my eyes. I mean, who smokes a cigarette while swimming? But there it is, dangling loosely from his lips, only inches away from the surface.

"Sorry," I mumble, realizing that my splash must have threatened to overtake it.

Without further incidents I fall into place and start moving in a smooth breast stroke. I pace the man at a distance of a couple of arm lengths as we go round and round, two hamsters in an slow-moving wheel, the only sound an occasional splash as an arm or a leg breaks the surface.

Soon I have lost count of how many times we've completed a new oval, but already after a few laps do I begin to feel clearer. By the time the man stops at the end of the one long straight and pulls himself up with the help of the ladder, I have let go of everything but my steady strokes and the sensation of water flowing over my body.

"Feels good, eh?"

The man doesn't look directly at me but shoots his words into thin air, and without waiting for my reply he begins a series of vigorous stretches by the side of the pool. I climb up the ladder and stand watching him. He's got a big belly and an old man's saggy skin that seems to be longing for the ground, the way it almost desperately pulls away from him. His face is scarred and haggard, but his legs are fine: muscular, not too stocky, but solid and strong. He twists and bends for several minutes, and when he is done he reaches for his towel on the floor in the corner and pulls from it a pack of cigarettes.

"You want one?" he says and offers me the open package, but only after first putting one in his own mouth.

"Thanks," I say, feeling a strange urge to comply.

The man lights both our cigarettes with smooth and elegant motions – I can tell he's done it a thousand times – and again reaches for his towel. This time he pulls a couple of beers from it, and I begin to wonder what else is hiding behind that towel of his. Perhaps Jimmy Hoffa?

He offers me a beer, and when I accept he looks at me in a way that finally acknowledges my existence.

"Without this," he says and takes a long sip from his can, "this would be torture," and he nods towards the pool. "With beer, swimming becomes a beautiful thing, like bobbing around in the world's largest cunt."

I take a sip and accidentally almost burn my eyebrow off with the glowing cigarette.

"So what's your story, kid?"

"Say again?" I say, wondering if he already knows about how I won the competition. Only when he continues do I get it.

"Where you from kid?"

Of course. He wants to know which book I'm from. I think about it for a second, then, with a smile I can't suppress, I say.

"The last book in the world."

We sit in the steam room, where we both become dim-featured, scary-looking figures of distorted proportion. We are dismembered – only a piece of a shoulder shows through the fog, an elbow, the tips of our noses, and the anonymity lets me relax in the company of my newfound, although slightly eccentric, friend. He's brought in two packs of beer that stands hidden somewhere in the whiteness below, and every now and then I can hear the pop from an opened can, once, twice, three times, and more, while I'm still sipping on my second. And every time the sound surprises me just as much.

We make small talk. Actually, he is the one who does the talking; I mostly listen, except when I answer his questions.

"What's the name?"

"Jonathan Butter," I say, now that I've become accustomed with the way he speaks.

"Tell you, Jonathan, I know I can bite the paper worth a damn, I'm not worried about that. What it is that nips at my gut like it was caught on barbed wire is the fear that I am not worried. Worried men who become unworried lose their blood faster than a chicken without a head, and then words no longer bite, but slither like shit all over a glossy magazine. Like old Hem getting his old man in the sea piece into *Life* because he figured out the formula."

The beer cans keep popping in the fog. I am half here, half gone, my body soaked in heat, the steam packed like dry ice up to the very tip of my nose. The whiteness is so thick that when I try to put my can down on the ledge right beside me I have to feel blindly for it. I'm on my third – my brain is sagging somewhat – nevertheless, I have it figured out: I'm with the great Buk, C. B., Henry Chinaski, Mr. Charles Bukowski himself.

"I'm one of those rare breeds that exist in two places. At least, I once did. I wrote myself straight into immortality."

A loud belch, which seems to go on forever and leaves a trail of beer breath in the steam, punctuates his words. He continues.

"They call us doubles, the creator and the created. You figure it out. Out there was a different game; here, drinking won't kill me and sadly, that's taken something from it. When the acid threatened to eat through the water balloon of life, I was on a wire. And it made my heart shriek and my balls tingle. Now I simply drink to quench my thirst and because that's how my hand moves."

Bukowski's voice trickles through the fog at a steady pace. *The man talks the same way he swims*, I think. The popping cans punctuate time, and the occasional belch is only a meaningless marker in the otherwise white oblivion. Bukowski has lots to say.

"I suppose that's the trouble with professional writers. They become so professional they stop living. I mean, they live as writers but stop living haphazardly as humans."

Whatever comes to him exits right through his mouth, without contemplation.

"Although I no longer live on one candy bar a day, life still kicks my ass pretty hard, mostly in the form of people, mostly in the form of women. Have had the flu and my balls actually ache and my woman is crying for sex, sex, sex. The gods are still playing with me."

Subjects ranging from high to low, his voice keeps grinding through the steam.

"It is our own death that will be easiest to take, it is the other deaths, the coming of them, that we cannot bear. I have tried to think myself gone, but it did not help. The wind cannot override itself. The wind is only a recent development. The instinct was there long before. When love burns to the ground it is both bitter and sweet. My mother died of cancer, my old man with the tap running. Jane had her guts hanging from her mouth. To say that I understand the machinery of it would be a lie. You know as much as I. Death is eternally everywhere, except here."

I hang onto the last sentence, because after it there follows no other. Only silence and the soft sweeping of the fog – there's not even the pop of another can. But just as I am about to reach out to touch Buk's foot to see if he is still here, his voice returns.

"You didn't think I only wanted you for your company, did you? I can spot a visitor a mile away."

It takes a while for me to absorb and understand the last sentence, my beer-soaked mind somewhat limp and sluggish.

"I need your help, and I know you need mine. Whatever it is you are doing here, I can help. I know this place inside and out. Remember, I used to be like you."

I'm slow to react to the fact that it's my turn, and when I finally speak I don't recognize my own voice. The words are in a jumble.

"I have thish lisht. I need to vishit them all, one by one. Then I can go home. But I can't becaushe I don't know what they look like."

"Well, god damn, kid, then I am your man. Even though I only understood half of what you just said, I know the face of every cat in this place, and where most of them drink. Because I drink in them all. You just name the names and I'll point the finger."

"Schanks," I say, suddenly feeling a strong love for this kind old man.

"But there's one thing you have to do for me."

"Schuure," I say, and I mean it.

"You have to kill me." Suddenly the fog and the heat becomes too much; the beer in my belly rises higher and higher, the tap broken off, until it shoots from my mouth, into the whiteness, and land with a *splosh* on the invisible floor.

"I am one half of a double caught forever between the covers of my own creations, and I need you to kill me."

When I have rested for a while, sitting on the bottom ledge with my head between my knees, I feel better. Down here the fog is no longer unbearably thick; I can see the outlines of the tiles on the floor, my knees, my legs, and my feet – even the softened edges of the wall across the room have become visible. Buk is still up in the deeper fog and I listen to his voice with a newfound clarity.

"I can't drink myself to death, I can't sit at the bottom of the pool – it's all make-believe. I am tired of it. One life is enough. More than enough. It's fine for the others, the ones that are born into it, but us doubles, we know about the other world."

Desperation has crept into his voice, and even though I can't see him, it is as if he is reaching out his hand through the fog.

"I need to get my shadow back where it belongs. Help me with this, and I will help you get out of this place."

It surprises me that I don't need to think about it. I already know my answer. It's easy. He isn't real. Nothing here is.

"Okay," I say, "just tell me what to do."

Back in the changing room I can finally get a good look at him again. I can read it in his eyes; they've seen it all a thousand times and now have only one wish. Buk treats the whole matter with perfect dignity and makes me swear on my heart to honor my promise.

"A man is only as good as his word," he says, and I secretly examine the scars on his face.

He lets me know that when the time is right, when I have done what I have to do and I'm ready to go home, he will let me know the details of his termination. That's the word he uses, *termination*. It strikes me as queer, but I don't say anything about it. Instead I pull the list from my pants and begin explaining the mess I've gotten myself into.

Buk's reaction isn't exactly what I had expected. He seems to think that my story is perfectly normal, as if he'd heard it a million times before. "Half of these I know where they are right now. Hell, I even know what they are drinking. The other half I will find. Hey ho, let's go, time's a wastin'." And that's all he has to say about it.

And with an energy and determination I wouldn't have expected from an old drunk with countless beers under his vest, Buk gets dressed and coaxes me to do the same. When we are ready he puts one hand on my shoulder and leads us out to the fourth floor lobby.

"You'll love this first fellow," he says and laughs, and I think I can even see a sparkle in his watery eye.

10

We arrive at a futuristic-looking bar with many sharp angles and a small tower of illuminated plastic boxes that slowly pulsate with warm colors. The brass plate reads Bar Futuro, and the purple carpet ends by the door. Inside, the floor is made of two-foot squares that light up, doubling in brightness when you step on them.

"This place always gives me a headache, but the bartender shakes up a martini so clean and clear that it immediately brings me back to zero again," Buk says.

I follow him to the bar, and I get the feeling we are off to see some wonderful Technicolor wizard. Having recently emptied my stomach, I'm more than happy when we have finally crossed the twinkling ocean and I can anchor myself in motionlessness.

While Buk orders – nothing for me, I'm officially on the wagon – I look around the bar. What strikes me is how the ice cream parlor and the smoking room seem to have the same exact layout as Bar Futuro. Even though this place is smooth and bulky – reminds me of an enormous melting ice cube – I get the feeling the bars are only set pieces in a studio. As if there is only the one room that gets rearranged to serve each purpose. I am just about to ask Buk about it when I feel his elbow.

"There's your man, hombre. Second from the end," and he leans back and downs his martini with one fast twitch of his hand.

I peer past Buk at the man. I don't want to ask, not yet, and try to connect the character with a destination on my list. He looks like an all-American feller, sporting a square jaw, vigilant eyes, and the stance of a brawling boxer, but with an air of refinement – or perhaps it's despair. He seems not to care about drinking at a bar in the middle of the day, or about anything at all. He just stares deeply into nothing and moves his jowl, prickled with a day's worth of stubble, as he finishes his drink.

"He's leaving! Hurry!"

Buk throws back another martini, and I am amazed by the fact that I never see where the olive goes. But there's no time to talk about the whereabouts of olives now.

"Hurry!" Buk wheezes and pulls me along.

The man grabs a hat and a coat from a hat rack that I must say looks far from futuristic, and steps into the corridor with them still in his hands. We run the last bit to catch up, and in the jumble Buk drops a martini glass to the floor, where it shatters. *How many martinis is he holding in that rabbit-holed body of his?* I have time to think as we fly into the hallway.

"Hold that door, gringo!"

Buk manages to jam his hand in the closing gap just in time.

"Going down?" he pants, and the man nods coolly.

The ride, however short, is filled with the tense silence only an elevator stocked with strangers can produce. Nobody says a word, and we all watch the light above the door. When the elevator finally comes to a halt, Buk holds me back and invites the man to be the first to leave.

"After you, mister," and together we watch him disappear through the heavy front doors.

Buk leans in so close I can feel the alcohol on his breath. He talks fast.

"You have a minute. He always gets his coat and hat on outside – can't go back without them now, could he? – and lights a cigarette on the street corner."

Buk carefully opens the door and peeks outside.

"There he goes. Now follow him. Hurry! Hurry!"

He pushes me onto the sidewalk, and I spot my mark, now wearing the trench coat and the hat, crossing the street towards the subway service entrance. I start after him, but then it strikes me that Buk's totally forgotten something.

"Name?" I whisper.

"Marlowe, baby. Private dick, Philip Marlowe."

Buk winks his eye at me but only manages to look drunk, and with this less-than-reassuring image to send me off, I hurry across the street and make it into the entrance just before the door slams shut behind Marlowe. Through the corridors I follow him as closely as I dare, tracking the sound of his footsteps, and when I hear yet another door slam shut I wait thirty seconds before I cross to the other side.

Right from the start, I know that I'm in L.A. I know because as I step from the shadowy tunnel and find myself on the sidewalk of a street lined with houses and palm trees, right above my nose, traversing the rolling hills like some giant caterpillar, are the white letters of the Hollywood sign. I feel pretty good, focused and relaxed, confident that I will be able to stay out of trouble for the required twenty-four hours. But I have only taken a few steps before I feel a hand come down heavily on my shoulder. I spin around and stand eye to eye with Marlowe.

"Good day," he says and looks at me sternly, his meaty extremity weighing me down.

Even if I wanted to, the sheer mass of it would have kept me from running.

"Good day," I say, my mind racing in search of a believable story.

"Are you following me?"

Marlowe pulls his eyebrows together into a solid brow, pinning me with his stare. For a moment his grip hardens, and I panic.

"It's not what you think."

"It never is," Marlowe says with a smile, and his grip finally loosens.

It's ten to five when he pulls up and parks close to the apartment building on Randall Place. A radio is bleating in the dark, and as Marlowe kills the engine the tunes from the radio pops, for a moment the only sound in the city, and I am bewitched by the solitude of it.

Marlowe greets me with a silent nod – he told me to be here exactly at ten to, and he would take me through the night till next morning – and I follow him into the building, trying to walk within the frame of his wide shoulders. I picture myself in a trench coat and hat, and considering the fact that I am about to enter a private eye's investigation in late-thirties Hollywood, I don't have to pretend very hard to convince myself of the illusion.

For the second time we get into an elevator together, and for the second time we don't say a word. But the awkward tension is gone. Instead I feel at ease, like a disciple trotting after his master, knowing that he is in the care of an expert.

We ride up to the fourth floor and walk down a rather narrow hall. A mild breeze is blowing in through the fire escape at one end.

"What should *I* do?"

I ask this in a hushed voice as we stop in front of a door marked 405. It has suddenly occurred to me that I have no idea what my purpose is. Nothing about this place rings a bell. But Marlowe seems not the least bit concerned, as if he's done it a thousand times before.

"Just do as I say," he grunts and pushes the doorbell.

Minutes pass – at least that's how it feels – and my heart is racing. But I keep it under control. I try to recall the details of the story, the who and the what and the when, but all I can conjure before the door opens is that there are several murders, all of which somehow lead back to the oil-wealthy Sternwood family. Then the hinges squeak.

I can't really see his face – Marlowe is blocking my view – but as he looks us over, the silence speaks of hostility more than any words could.

"Geiger?" It's Marlowe who finally breaks the tension.

The tone of his voice reveals that he knows it's not really Geiger, but the question needs to be asked. The man who is not Geiger keeps quiet. A puff of smoke comes from behind the door, where it stops briefly before it divides in two parts around Marlowe, only to come together again behind his wide back.

"You said what?"

The man's voice is cool and unbothered.

"Geiger. Arthur Gwynn Geiger."

Now I remember. Geiger is the guy with the smut books.

"Don't know anybody by that name," the voice continues. Is it my imagination, or is his composure ever so slightly disturbed?

Marlowe continues to ask questions and first when he eventually leans forward against the door and says something about a *sucker list* to the mysterious man, who apparently is called Joe, I realize I don't have the guts to be a private dick. All I want is to go home. But then the door opens wide and Marlowe disappears inside, and I have no choice but to follow.

I nod to the man called Joe. He's got a dark complexion and dark brown eyes that look me over without expression, and he doesn't nod back. In that glimpse of a moment I can't help but wonder about his character, if he too drinks at the Once Upon a Time Palace Café, if he too walks back and forth through the subway service entrance. But my thoughts about his other, leisurely life, vanish as he closes the door firmly behind me.

We step right into a sort of sitting room. Marlowe is already seated on a davenport. The dark fellow, Joe, comes in behind me and plods straight over to a large, wooden desk studded with thick black nails, without looking at either Marlowe or at me. I find myself standing halfway between them, in front of a set of French windows that open up onto a stone porch. Joe props himself on a chair opposite us, and only when he puts a cigar to his mouth do I see the box in his lap.

"Cigar?" he says and holds up one the size of a small cucumber.

Without waiting for a reply he tosses it at Marlowe, who instinctively reaches for it, and just as Marlowe catches the flying roll of tobacco, Joe has pulled out a gun. He holds it directed at Marlowe, but I feel the probing gaze of the black-eyed barrel all the same.

I get ready to run. I go over it in my head; if I thrust myself through the windows I can roll away across the porch and drop to the ground from the edge. But there's something about the situation that makes me unable to move. Joe begins to deliver one tough-guy line after another, while Marlowe, on the other hand, looks quite at ease – as you would be, I guess, if guns were pointed at you every day. Without flinching, he ignores Joe's order for him to stand up.

"You're the second guy I've met within hours who seem to think a gat in the hand means a world by the tail."

I have to hand it to Chandler, he knew how to write the bloody one-liners. And Marlowe does his job delivering them. But the gun looks very real, and I suspect the bullet that comes out of it makes an equally real hole, so I immediately abandon my lionhearted porch escape.

The two of them go at it back and forth for a moment, Joe's eyes mean at first but cooling off little by little. But I don't listen to their words. All I can do is stare at the pointed black slipper sticking out from under the curtain that hangs over the doorway.

Apparently I'm not the only one noticing them, because suddenly Joe calls out "Agnes," and out steps a woman. She's a blonde, with thighs that run from the floor up to her armpits, and she looks at Marlowe, then at me, and her glance is dark and vicious.

"I knew damn well you were trouble," she hisses and glares at Marlowe. "And who the hell is this?"

She walks by me, close enough to reach out and bite my nose off, and I pull back as far as I can without falling through the windows.

"Just an extra, don't mind him." Marlowe says, while his eyes remain locked on Joe.

"Save the gags," Joe says and orders the blonde to turn on the light.

With a defiant sigh she does as she is told, then sinks into a chair beside the lamp, where her hair assumes a soft glow.

Marlowe starts talking about a list of names, but halfway through I stop listening and find myself staring at the blonde's legs and the gun in Joe's hand. They're all I really care about.

At one point the blonde breaks out in a gargle of words, quite upset by something Marlowe has said, but it quickly subsides into a gasping simmer. Then Marlowe says something that turns *my* spine to ice.

"You shot Geiger to get it. Last night in the rain. It was dandy shooting weather."

The last thing I want is to get caught in the middle of a shootout between these two. I desperately try to think of ways to excuse myself and leave without getting shot in the process. Meanwhile, the mouthing continues. Up until now Joe had looked mighty upset – about ready to burst – but in the next moment it seems that all the air has gone out of him. He relaxes the gun to his knee, and I see my chance.

"I forgot something," I say and start towards the front door.

Instantly Marlowe's voice is there, deep and commanding. "Ya stay right here."

As if on a cue – it might as well have been a Broadway play – the buzzer rings. Thrown off course by the bombilation, I obediently go back to my spot in front of the windows. And it's there I stand, fumbling with my memory, trying to recall what is coming next, as Joe walks backwards into the room with a small revolver pressed against his lips. The penny drops – it's Carmen Sternwood.

She looks pale and unhealthy, small but strangely well-proportioned, and her grey eyes are directed not at Marlowe nor at me, but at Joe.

"I want my pictures, Joe," she demands, and only now do I notice that Marlowe is struggling with the blonde. A loud snap turns my attention back to Carmen and Joe, who are wrestling on the floor, before Marlowe's laughter brings my eyes back to the other end of the room. It's now Marlowe who holds a gun, and in a few quick and skillful moves he has them all rounded up. With one hand he grabs me by the shoulder and leads me across the room, standing me in the hallway.

"In case anyone tries to run," he says and winks one eye at me.

I see Joe handing something to Marlowe, and immediately Carmen claws for it.

"I'll take care of them for you. Go on home." Marlowe is unbending.

He opens the front door and waits for Carmen to pass me on her way out. She grins in despair, showing me a row of sharp little teeth.

When Carmen is gone, Marlowe continues with Joe, picking it up from where he was interrupted. He tells me to stay put – I really don't want to, but I don't have the guts to go against Marlowe.

They talk about Carmen, about the books and that fellow Geiger's murderer. I'm not sure how long it goes on, but my back has begun to ache when the buzzer rings again.

"That bitch." Joe says bitterly and takes a step towards the door, but Marlowe holds him back.

"Would you get that, pal?" he says to me.

I walk over to the door, put my hand on the knob, expecting to be reunited with Carmen's face. But am I ever surprised. Staring into my eyes is a good-looking young man with slick black hair. And am I ever surprised when he calls me by another name.

"Brody?"

And am I even more surprised when he presses a gun to my chest and pulls the trigger.

The explosions are muffled, but it's not the noise that I notice the most, it's the expression of surprise sweeping across the young man's face. When he turns around and runs down the hallway I sink to the floor, first to my knees, then onto my back, his face the only image I hold in my mind. The door slowly swings shut, but not all the way, for my hand is caught between it and the post. The next thing I know Marlowe is standing over me, glaring first at my chest and then my face.

"Sorry, kid," he says, but I don't understand what for.

He then takes one step right over me and disappears out through the door, which again falls shut over my hand.

There's no pain – I can feel the holes with my fingers – but the pain is nowhere to be found. They are round and sharp-edged, the holes, as if punched through with a power drill. Joe comes up to me with the most curious look on his face. I hardly recognize him, and when he starts talking I don't pay any attention to his words because at that point I can hear the much sweeter sound of sirens wailing in the distance. Soon the door fills with policemen in navy-blue uniforms that look hot and heavy, then with ambulance drivers wearing white that looks light and cool. I decide that I'd rather go with them. They all crouch down next to me, pressing gauze to my chest, and then I am hoisted from the ground and put on a stretcher. On my way out I finally pick up what Joe keeps repeating, over and over again.

"It was supposed to be me. It was supposed to be me."

Stars emerge – yellow chunks of neon flung high upon a dark blue sky, and I watch them, all the way down the fire escape, until the roof of the ambulance cuts them from my sight. One man stays with me in the back and continues to press rags into my holes, but it still doesn't hurt. I feel so little I begin to wonder whether I was really shot, or if I am somehow immortal. But at the hospital, as I am hoisted from the stretcher in the ambulance to another stretcher waiting outside, the pain catches up with me. The stars are still out, but they are now razor-sharp slivers of white glass embedded deep in my chest. They roll me through a corridor, and I have the urge to find out what color carpet covers the floor, only to discover that it hurts too much to even lift my head. I am taken into a bright white room where a rubber mask swallows my face and pulls me down, down to the bottom where everything is completely dark and tranquil.

Marlowe is by my side when I wake up. His face is covered in stubble, more than a day's worth, and he looks down at me with anxious eyes.

"How you feelin', kid?"

I don't know where I am, so my repsonse is automatic, "Fine."

Then I remember. I was shot.

"I was shot." I say.

"I know it, kid, and it was my fault. But listen, we have to get out of here. Can you walk?"

Marlowe doesn't wait for my reply and slides his hands under my armpits – there's an urgency in the way he looks at me, and it's enough for me not to ask. My chest aches something awful, and only with Marlowe's help do I finally manage to get up.

"I know it hurts, but we have to move quickly."

With these foreboding words Marlowe gently leads me towards the door. He looks both ways before pulling me into the hallway, and I think it's a strange thing to do but say nothing. It is morning, judging by the sharpness of the light through the windows, the way it will burn cold and clear until the afternoon when it will begin its slow fade into red. I wheeze and feel like coughing, but I know that if I do the pain will be even worse, so I hold it back. Marlowe presses the elevator call button one, two, three, four times, and once inside he does the same to make the doors close. This is now our third time together in an elevator, I realize, but we still don't say a word.

The car is parked by the curb just outside the entrance. Marlowe leads me to the passenger side, opens the door, and waits until I have eased myself onto the seat – slowly, as one would ease into a very hot bath – before he rushes around the car and leaps in behind the wheel.

"What's wrong?" I ask and turn my head carefully to glance the other way, at the hospital, as if the answer lies there. And just as Marlowe mouths his words, my mind plays a trick on me: I think I see part of the facade fold in half and fall to the ground.

"She's crumbling," he says and steps hard on the gas.

We drive in haste through the city, and I have to muster all my strength to sit as still as possible. Even so, every sharp turn sends nerve-shattering pain through my chest, and every crease in the road clenches my teeth. Marlowe drives faster and faster, and I can cast only half an eye on the world swooshing by outside the window. At this speed, through the haze of pain, it really does look as if every other house is falling apart.

"What's the big rush?" I manage to squeeze out between my tightened lips.

Marlowe keeps driving, his head stretched forward a foot in front of his body, concentration a furry knot between his brows. Without warning, he slams on the brakes and we come to a skidding halt.

"We have to get out of here, right now."

I consider his matter-of-fact tone as I watch him get out and run around the car to my side.

"Quickly, quickly!"

He lifts me out with his two large hands supporting my armpits. At first I don't know where we are, but then I look up and see the sign crawling across the hills above. We're back at the beginning.

The pain when Marlowe suddenly pushes me to the ground is sharp and blinding. I take a deep breath and let it run through me, and when I open my eyes and let the world back in, I see a chunk of brick the size of a bulldog on the sidewalk. It seems that that one piece of brick and mortar was what I needed to wake up, for at once I see buildings crumbling all around us.

"Wha…"

I don't get a chance to even formulate the question before Marlowe violently drags me into the driveway. There, only a couple of steps from the garage, the ground bulges and we both nearly fall down again, but Marlowe pulls me along, and before I even register the pain in my chest we are standing inside.

The garage is almost empty except for a few shelves stacked with bowling pins, rakes, and an assortment of bottles. The only light comes from a small side window high up on the wall, and in the darkness a murky smell lingers. The ground shakes again, sending a heavy rain of something hard against the roof. After the cacophony there follows an eerie silence, then a thunderous crash sets the entire building shaking.

"Hurry!" Marlowe bellows.

He scuttles forward to the middle of the garage where he bends down and jerks open a hatch in the floor. A ladder leads down into a dark pit, and he doesn't have to tell me twice to start climbing. A multitude of loud crashes pelts us from above, and when I hear the hatch slam shut

I hurry down the last steps to make room for Marlowe. I breathe hard; I stand on the floor in the damp stone tunnel and wait for him. I look up into the darkness of the shaft until it doesn't make sense to wait any longer, but there is no one behind me. I call out his name, and when I get no reply I decide I have to, despite the pain in my chest.

It's so dark that I only know I've reached the top when I hit my head on the underside of the hatch. It isn't the hollow thud I had expected, but rather the sound of pummeling a solid stone wall. There is no way I will be able to open it.

I bang it with my fist in frustration, and... there, through the darkness comes a faint voice!

"Hurry...the tunnel..."

It's Marlowe! Then once again, this time aching with urgency, "Hurry!"

Without thinking, my mind accustomed to doing whatever Marlowe's stern voice demands, I slide back down, not caring that my insides feel ripped apart by every movement. I scuffle forward through the tunnel as fast as I can – I am half running, half walking – while the lightbulb's ominous flicker threatens to engulf me in complete darkness.

I no longer care about the pain in my chest or about the sour taste in the back of my throat. I only care about getting through the tunnel and back into the not quite real, but stable enough, world of the Palace. I put one foot in front of the other, swing my arms back and forth, and not until I throw myself against the last door do I let go of everything and fall facedown on the ground.

I lie where I am without moving. The world is turned sideways; yellow cabs drive straight up into the sky and straight down into the ground, and the tops of buildings spike out to the sides from a wall of cement, reaching for a wall of light blue. I do what I can to ease the pain and breathe only when absolutely necessary. This seems to do the trick for, eventually, I feel clearheaded enough to sit up.

I brace myself for it, but, to my utter surprise, there is no pain. It even fails to pounce on me as I draw a couple of deep breaths. And when I push myself up on all fours I don't feel much at all. I stand up and run my fingers over my chest, inside my white hospital robe, fumbling across the bandaged surface. I bend my body in every direction, I jump and I squat, never having felt better in my life. Finally I push my fingers behind the bandages in search of the bullet holes, and I can't belive it. My wounds are gone.

I have to search for a long time before I finally find him sitting at the end of the long bar in a place called the ABC Room. He has a score of empty glasses grouped in front of him, on which he looks down at with an empty stare. The ABC Room seems to be the kind of place where empty glasses and empty stares are part of the decor. A few other guests sit alone and unspeaking by their tables, each with their hoard of beer mugs, flutes, and highball glasses. I wonder why the bartender doesn't take them away, but then I notice the wall behind the bar; there is a chalkboard cluttered with names and numbers, and I realize it is some sort of tally. I've come across the Olympians of drinking.

I sidle up next to Buk and clear my throat. When he doesn't move I say, this time a bit louder, "Who's winning?"

This appears to go through to him, and he slowly turns his head my way. I say his head because that's the only thing that moves; like an owl's caput, it spins on its own axle until our eyes meet.

"I'm up two on Ignatius Reilly."

His face is bloated and red, and I decide to hold my questions at least until he has sobered up somewhat. But just like that, as if only pretending, he snaps out of his starry-eyed glare and stands up quicker than a soldier. With a voice loud and clear, ringing of life, he declares, "Let's go to the pool."

The pool is empty but for the two of us. We swim in silence, me behind Buk, whose cigarette becomes a tugboat's smoking chimney pushing through the sea. Once again I lose count of how many times we go around, and once again I am taken by surprise when it's over. All of a sudden I see Buk's wide back, covered in deep, craterlike scars, ascending the ladder.

In the corner, with Buk swinging back and forth in his violent stretching routine, it seems we walk in our own footsteps, tracing each of our previous movements, playing back a tape. I try to get a line in – I am bursting with questions – but Buk hushes me before I can say a word.

A couple of beers later, surrounded by steam so thick we could shave it off our arms and legs with a razor, I finally break through to him.

"What happened in there? They shot me, then the world fell apart and Marlowe was trapped."

I had planned to ask one question at the time and hold out for a satisfying answer before continuing, but instead they all come at once. Not that it much matters, Buk only cracks open another beer and begins talking about something entirely different.

"Funniest thing I ever heard, or I wouldn't call it funny but I will since I just did, although I'd rather call it the oddest, was this here woman poetess-editor who was putting out this piece about convict poets. She was mighty disturbed over the fact that 'all they seemed to write was about wanting to get out of jail.' Oh this cowardly cunt, if she had ever been trapped within four walls, not able to see the stars, go to the movies, or even down the block to buy cigarettes, if she could only have been forced to walk back and forth, hither and thither, without going anywhere, day in and day out, until her womb grew cold and cement-hard and she realized she would never be in no other room unless death or pardon put her there. This cunt of a woman, or anyone that has never been trapped, could ever understand the trapped and their endless trampling."

I want to let his words dissolve and disappear in the vapour before I try my questions on him again – this time I don't want anything to muddle my answers. I sit silent, anticipating the right moment, but just as the time is right Buk begins again with his fabulations.

"Yeah, sweetheart, life is a spider, we can only dance in the web so long. The thing is gonna get us, you know that."

There is a short pause before he continues.

"I don't mix too well with other people, I never have. Just don't know what to say to them. They yammer and I only sit there, feeling foolish and dumb. They come up with lots of action, jazz, life, and I may like them, but I can't contribute. Really, hell, there's nothing to say. There's been too much of everything. I am a loner. Just because I'm here, just because, doesn't mean I have scope or any such damn thing. I sense that other people touch each other, they belong, but I've never belonged. I'm sliced off forever. Blighted goddamned roaring stinking world. Now cheer up."

It is hard to follow the incessant rambling streaming out from the whiteness. I'm not sure if it even means anything, or if it's a metaphor for the way of the world, but he cracks open yet another beer and I wait for the gurgling of it flowing down his throat to stop. I make myself ready. It takes forever, but when it finally stops, punctuated by an almost equally long burp, Buk beats me to it again. His voice is so calm and slow, as if deep thoughts lie behind his words.

"There are people, out there" – I gather he means behind the doors in the corridors, behind the subway service entrance – "who think there is a way out. Not all of them, not even many, thank god, but a few select. They will see right through you, chumps like Marlowe with more than peas for a brain, and they will do anything to get out."

Confused, I try hard to understand.

"But the truth, what they don't know, is that there is no way out. Not for them. Ever. Only for people like me and you."

My questions are now in disarray, and I grab at what I can.

"But what happened to Marlowe? I saw houses crumble to pieces!"

Buk lets out a laugh that quickly turns into a coughing fit. When he is done panting for air he continues.

"What you saw was real, but still part of the show. You aren't sporting those bullet holes anymore, are you? Marlowe and the houses will be fine. The story will start from the beginning again, just like a dream after you wake up for a piss in the middle of the night."

"So it's all a dream in there then?"

I want to understand, but everything that has happened to me lately...A dream I could understand.

"I guess you can say that. A dream that plays over and over again."

And with that, question time is finished and I hear him get up. If I hadn't known better, I might have been scared by his huffing and puffing, monstrous by itself, as he moves across the floor towards the door.

"But don't get any bullets in more vital parts, compadre, or you'll stay behind," Buk announces before I hear the door slam shut and I am left all alone.

I stare into the whiteness, hard and unflinching, until tears overtake my vision. The terror of being shot finally catches up with me, and yet it's an unwarranted fear because here I am, unharmed. I close my eyes and wipe away my tears, and when I open them again I find that the whiteness is staring right back at me. I feel myself lift off my seat, levitating for a moment, before I sink back to the wet tiles. The face is one I know all too well by now. Koob.

"Did I frighten you, my dear Jonathan?"

Koob is as cheerful and polite as ever, but I am not too pleased to see him.

"Have you come to gloat? Or perhaps change the rules again?"

In the steam, without the chimney for a nose and the burning orifice of a mouth, Koob's features are softer, more angelic.

"Not at all dear Jonathan, not at all. On the contrary – I've come to warn you."

"Warn me?"

My question is as much a challenge for Koob to go on with his ridiculousness. I just can't trust him.

"Well, yes, it seems you ran into a bit of a problem in the last story."

"Problem? No problem."

My answer cuts him off but doesn't silence him.

"Well, the *problem* I am referring to is the meddling. I specifically told you not to meddle with the stories. There's just no telling what can happen if you do."

Suddenly I've had enough of both the steam room and Koob's malicious warnings. I refuse to be drawn into any more of his games. He's done enough. Whenever he appears, something bad happens and I am the one to suffer for it. *Well, let's just see how he likes to be on the receiving end of the stick.*

I get up and walk through the mist with outstretched hands. I hear Koob's voice behind my back.

"Jonathan, this is a serious matter."

I open the door but I don't leave. Instead I stand and watch the steam well out through the doorway, and it isn't long until it's thinned out so much I can make out the wall at the opposite end. Koob's voice, now weaker, is pleading with me.

"Jonathan! Listen to me!"

But I am done listening. I hold the door open until all the steam is gone and Koob's voice and features have vanished completely. From now on I will only trust myself and Buk. And little by little, just like the steam, I will trickle through the walls of this other world.

11

Buk is on the bench in the changing room, studying the list intently.

"Aha!" he says triumphantly just as I walk in, and flicks a knuckle against the paper. "This one's easy to find. Seamen, they walk like they're drunk even when they're not. My kind of people. Quickly, get dressed so we can catch this son of a bitch before the show begins."

In a fisherman's gloomy bar, one floor below ground, where lanterns hanging from the low ceiling are the only source of light, and old fishing nets, complete with glass floats, hang on the wall behind the bar, Buk and I sit watching the man I am about to follow. Gray-bearded and leather-skinned, he looks as salt as any man can get, and when he steps out of the bar with a nod to the bartender, it is only another second until I have him figured out.

This time we ride down in separate elevators, so as not to jeopardize my identity, and when the elevator door opens we run to the front door. But there's no rush. The wooden leg has relentlessly held him back.

Captain Ahab looks for a break in traffic long enough for him to dare make the leap, and when one appears, he hobbles towards the subway service entrance.

"Go get him, kid," Buk says and sends me off with a hearty slap on the back.

I step through the last door and, to my surprise, find myself in steep darkness. It's an oily, pitchy blackness, but the longer I stand there the more it dilutes into a lucid sort of dark in which the soft contours of fabric create an alley leading up, over a creaky and uneven wooden floor, to yet another door. Cobweb-thin rays of light seep through the crack above it, but they are so dim I still have to feel with my hands for the lock. It's a closet, I realize and I step out into a room.

The room is small, cold as a clam, and furnished with a bed the size of a lifeboat. Present company excluded, it's empty of people and I take a few careful steps towards the middle, each and every one of which creaks madly. An old sea chest that doubles as a washstand stands in one corner, and over by the fireplace hangs a rude shelf littered with bonefish hooks and, in the middle, a dark painting of a man striking a whale with his harpoon. The squeaks of an opening door, then the sudden loudness of it slamming shut, breaks the silence. I hurry over to the window just in time to see Captain Ahab limp on down the street, into the darkness.

Outside I discover it's freezing, and I run back into the house, up the stairs and back to the closet, where I equip myself with coat, gloves, and a thick sweater before I hurry down, double-speed, into the street again. I sprint after Ahab. It's not long before I spot him – the town doesn't appear to be very large, and Ahab is walking slowly on that leg of his.

The darkness is of the early-morning kind, peculiarly lit because of a fog. It is impossible to see objects clearly from more than a few feet away, however, it proves to be a blessing by keeping me out of Ahab's sight, even though at times it feels like we are only an arm's length apart.

The cold air nips at my cheeks, and I draw the coat tighter around my body. I follow the sound of Ahab's leg striking the cobbled stones until the air grows damper. The whiteness is thicker here by the water. I can hear the solemn lapping at land's edge, and without warning a big, dark, shapely thing swells out of the murkiness. This is my cue, and I stop where I am and let Ahab continue without me. She is the mythological one, the vessel steered through so many minds...the ship whose name I can't for the world seem to remember.

Twenty-four hours I am bound to stay, a day and a night. I could just trot back through the fog, follow the path forged by our passage, and wait upstairs in the large bed. Or I could find an inn, have a drink and listen to old seafarers' stories. Or I could just walk the streets until time is up and I have sufficient fare to go back. On the other hand – there's a quaint tickle in my soul – here I am, thrust into one of the greatest stories ever written, could I justify going back and hiding out in some old house? I know for a fact that the ship comes to no harm whatsoever within the first twenty-four hours. It will yet be many pages until the encounter with Moby Dick, and, until then, I am sure to be safe from danger: it's like being handed a piece of life for which you have already seen the scoreboard. I have twenty-four hours of risk-free living ahead of me. The tickle persists, and I decide I might as well enjoy this involuntary ride, despite its unfortunate beginning, and I begin walking towards the dark thing.

I wait a while before I board. She lies still and quiet as I walk slowly alongside her; it is really too dark yet to see her in detail, other than that she is a grand old wooden ship. *Fit for a pirate*, I think. I reach the very back of her and peer through the now-grey fog, trying hard to read her name. *Beyond*. It does not ring a bell. I'm positive it is something more savage, and as I lean forward from the harbor's edge as far as I dare, a slight breeze shifts the heaviness of the mist and in that moment the name flashes through: *Pequod*. That is her name indeed! With this I feel comfortable enough to step on board.

On deck it is profoundly quiet. Perhaps it's like the old saying, the calm before the storm, but I cannot recall any storm, at least not in these latitudes of the story.

Carefully I cross the deck to the front of the ship, upon where I find an open hatch. There's a light on below – I listen but hear not a breath from her depths – and I begin my descent, quickly calling to mind any old seaman's words and expressions that might come in handy. By good fortune my limited knowledge is never required, for the man that I find in the scuttle is sound asleep.

He is wrapped in a tattered jacket and lies full-length across two chests, facedown, with his chins buried deep into his folded arms. There is no place for me to sit but on the floor. I slide down against the wall and fold my arms across my drawn-up knees, and when I hear the voices and scuffles of others making their way down the ladder, I quickly close my eyes and pretend to be asleep.

"Those sailors we saw, Queequeg, where can they have gone to?" the one man says to the other. He has a fine voice and pronounces each word as if it was a gift of great value.

The other only grunts in reply as the first one continues at length about how they should wake the sailor up so that there is room for them all to sit. In the following silence, the grunting one grunts again, and curiosity tempts me to open my eyes for a peek. Just as I do, the first one bursts out, "Gracious! Queequeg, don't sit there!"

Another grunt precedes the other's actual reply: "Oh! Perry dood seat. My country way; won't hurt him face."

"Face!" says the first one, whom I by now have identified as Ishmael himself, the prodigious narrator.

"Call that his face? Very benevolent countenance then; but how hard he breathes, he's heaving himself. Get off, Queequeg, you are heavy. It's grinding the face of the poor… Get off, Queequeg! Look, he'll twitch you off soon. I wonder he don't wake!"

Queequeg is the savage, there's no doubt about that. I am astounded to see him before me: a big muscular body, covered in tattoos, hardened with the kind of weathered tan that will never fade away. He has pulled his hair up and fastened it at the very top with laces, just like a sumo wrestler, and his eyes are dark but very clear.

I find it safest to close my eyes again and just listen. They talk about Queequeg's home, how it is common there for noblemen to sit on men of lesser stature – at least that's what I figure from the little I understand of his broken English. When the air fills with a sort of sweet smoke, Ishmael breaks in with a question.

"What's that for, Queequeg?"

Queequeg answers excitedly, "Perry easy, kill-e; oh! Perry easy!"

I hope he means the man lying facedown across the chests, but just in case I rustle my legs and smack my lips a few times to make sure I'm not the one on the menu.

A saving grace perhaps, but a few moments later the sleeping man awakens.

"Hollowa, who be ye, smokers?" he says.

"Shipped men," answers Ishmael. Then he adds, "When does she sail?"

"Aye, aye, ye are going in her, be ye? She sails today. The captain is aboard."

"What captain? Ahab?"

"Who but him indeed?"

As if on cue there is commotion from the deck above, and all three men stir and quickly make their way up through the hatch. As soon as I hear their feet trample above me I open my eyes and join them, emerging into the sunrise that is just about to chase the fog away.

The crew is arriving on board in twos and threes, and soon everyone is engaged in some sort of task. I try to blend in and join the line that brings onboard the last things from shore; I take a parcel from the man in front of me and hand it to the man behind, and so on.

The hours pass quickly in this way, and nobody asks my name or what I am doing on board, so I figure they have simply taken me for another hired mate. When the last goods are stored, the ship takes leave of the harbor by loosening the ropes that had it tethered there. All in all, I think it is a rather withered departure, this being, after all, the ship that is to chase after the infamous white whale. But I quickly settle my disappointment, for we only go a little bit out into the bay before the anchor plunges into the dark sea with a solid splash.

There is a pause in the activity, and I linger on deck. At last I have the chance to examine this spectacular craft. She is an old ship – perhaps she is top-of-the-line for her time – and I spot two other ships in the harbor – the *Devil-Dam* and the *Tit-bit* – which look, at least to my untrained eye, to be both younger and more modern. Weather-stained, no doubt by all four oceans, the *Pequod*'s complexion is as darkened as Queequeg's skin. The deck is worn and wrinkled but very smooth, sanded by a thousand bare feet walking it a thousand times over. Her two masts stand stiffly against the sky, but what draws my eyes mostly is that all around her bulwarks sit the sharp teeth of some animal. It makes the entire deck appear as the interior of a giant jaw. I touch one, but as soon as my hand runs across it, orders ring out and I race to comply.

"Aft here, ye sons of bachelors!" cries one man into the air. "Man the capstan! Blood and thunder! Jump!"

At his command many men run for what looks to be a cross made by four equally sturdy blocks of wood, and I hurry to join them. Each of us finds a spot on the cross – there are so many hands it's nearly impossible – and then we begin churning it around, pressing the full weight of our bodies behind it. After countless laps the ship quivers: there is no longer a tie between her and the open sea.

"Spring, thou sheep-head; spring, and break thy backbone!"

The man in charge spits his words over us, and we work the cross even harder. At last the anchor is all the way up. Meanwhile, the sails have been set, and it isn't long before we glide off.

Just like the night, the day is cold, and a freezing spray quickly ices over the sides of the ship. I follow a group of men around and mimic what they do, and before I know it hours have passed. Sea air fills my lungs to the brim and the salty oxygen is intoxicating; when I finally look up there is no longer any land in sight. Something about this worries me, something that sits perched at the edge of my brain, but however hard I try I can't shake it loose enough to come tumbling down into consciousness.

Daylight quickly withers, and soon the night is over us and the *Pequod* dips into the green, rolling hills of the sea, the wind howling so hard the ropes hum out a sorrowful tune. The freezing spray has encased the foredeck in ice, and the teeth shine like daggers in the moonlight.

I don't notice it until it is almost alongside us; a slim sailboat sidles up against our hull, both ships rocking wildly in the heaving sea, and the two men who've been screaming orders at us since sunrise climb over the edge, and with a farewell I can't hear from where I stand, drop into the sailboat. Ship and boat diverge, and just as they do a screaming seagull flies in between the two. At this the crew gives three hearty cheers, and that's when a sharp-knuckled realization smashes into my temple. The closet, how on earth will I get back to the closet!?

I react immediately. I haven't seen Captain Ahab yet, and with cold sweat running down my back, I run to the man I gather is the highest in command. I grab him by the arm and, rather violently, swing him to face me.

"Sir, we have to go back! The door, I need to step through the closet tomorrow!"

For a moment I think my words have gone through, but when the man rips his arm loose and gives me a hard kick in the ass, I know he will never understand. In panic I sprint to the back of the ship to see if I can spot the sailboat.

How could I be so stupid?! The *Pequod* is going out to stay out. A sigh escapes me when I see that the sailboat is still there. It disappears and reappears in the watery valleys, painted dark silver by the moonlight, but moving fast away from us. I shout and wave both my arms, but there is no response from the small craft. *The mast,* I think; I run to the closest one and without hesitation begin to climb up the ropes. Ice covers the twines more than halfway up, but my gloves, although bulky and stiff from the saltwater, give me enough grip to reach the top. From up here I can see the lantern of the sailboat dip into the dark hollows, and I clear my throat.

But it's no good, my voice trails off in the wind, a directionless offering to the sea. Carefully I pry one hand loose, lean forward so that my weight is up against the wood, then pry off the second. I sneak them up to my mouth, where I form a megaphone of flesh and wool, and just as I am about to fire through it my scream for help, the *Pequod* catches a wave and swings wildly to one side.

Even before I fall I know that I will; my one hand catches hold of the rope, but by then it is too late – I am already on the move and don't have enough strength to reverse it. For a moment I am floating, the dark water below appearing wild and threatening, and then, just like a bullet, I begin to tear through the air.

In the stretched-out seconds that follow, words from some unknown source fly from my lips. I can't imagine anyone interpreting them as anything but a cry of fear as I tumble towards the surface, but I myself hear them, and, even though I am seconds from a sure death, what enters my ears surprises me.

"This is just a story!" My voice is loud and authoritative.

And then I hit the water.

I torpedo down into the sea – I don't know how many feet, my eyes are closed – and when I stop moving towards the center of the earth I kick my legs as hard as I can. When I finally break the surface and open my eyes, I can't believe it. None of it.

First of all, it is broad daylight. The sun stands high in the sky – not a cloud in sight to challenge it – while the night that was here just seconds ago has been chased away. Secondly, the sea that was, if not raging, then at least throwing a maritime temper tantrum of green-backed waves garnished with frothing white teeth, is now calm as a clam. Not a ripple disturbs its blank surface. And how warm it is! The tropical sea – or my bathtub for that matter – couldn't have produced a more comfortable temperature than the tepid soup in which I now tread. The *Pequod* is right there, which means I am still in *Moby Dick*. I haven't been slung into another story or dimension. It is the same, yet everything about it is different.

Even the *Pequod* seems different. She sits there, perfectly still, and on her deck stands the entire crew, looking down at me with identical expressions across their faces – equal portions worry and disbelief, seasoned with more than a pinch of confusion. Nobody moves, and I start to feel rather uneasy with all that attention. For a fleeting moment the thought that I might give them a wave, just a small hello with one hand, pops into my mind. But then, from out of nowhere, comes my salvation in the shape of an O.

The rescue ring flies over everybody's heads in a well-shaped arch to land but a foot from me, and with that the spell is broken. The men begin to move about – I grab the ring and there is all of a sudden such activity on board, with men running in all directions, that I'm not sure I *want* to get on the *Pequod* just yet. But I have no choice. I am hauled in by the rope, and without a single stroke I arrive at the ship's side where a harness is lowered, and without really moving a finger, five minutes after I took the plunge, I am back on deck. A poor-looking creature, no doubt, soaked and disorderly, with water draining from my clothes, but alive.

The men have once again returned to silence, throwing almost shy glances my way. I don't say anything – I feel so heavy, my water-soaked coat weighing on my shoulders, pinning me to the deck – it's hard enough to just breathe. Besides, I wouldn't know what to say. I'm just about to wiggle out of my coat when I, from my seated position, watch as the men part and Captain Ahab limps forward through the opening.

"What is the meaning of this?" he demands with a dark frown.

His voice is, sort of, just what I had always expected, hard and wild, yet dignified in a way that lets you understand that he is no doubt harboring a great inner energy that eats at his soul and ignites his eyes. The only surprise is his accent; he has the thickest southern drawl imaginable, and it clashes wildly with the rest of him.

"Captain Ahab, I'm so sorry," I begin, but his hand comes up sharply and stops me before I can continue.

"Skip it," he says, "you can explain it to the Board."

With disbelief I see that in his hand he grasps the one thing I least expect to see in one of the classics of literature: with a confident movement, he presses a cellphone against his ear. "Ahab here. Come and get us."

His words are short and precise, and with them the men, including Ahab himself, scatter around deck, making themselves comfortable as it seems, as if preparing for a long wait. I stay where I am, too confused to even move. Eventually I manage to slip out of my coat and sit back against the railing, drying off under the warm sun. I can't say that I'm ready for the next strangeness, nevertheless, within the hour I hear the sound of them – motorboats.

At the approaching sound everybody gets up. What I see when I join the curious mass gazing over the railing are two shiny, knife-shaped powerboats howling out of the distance, cutting back on the engines only at the very last second. They glide the last short distance, sidling up with perfect precision along the *Pequod*. I am utterly confused. I turn to a man next to me and ask, "What is going on? How can there be motorboats?"

But he is either deaf or pretends not to have heard me, for he keeps silent. I look around for a friendly face. I spot Ishmael and Queequeg standing up near the front of the ship and hurry over.

"Ishmael!"

I reach him and lay a hand on his shoulder.

"Ishmael," I say, "what on earth is going on? Please tell me!"

Ishmael looks embarrassed and flicks his eyes from side to side. I think he won't speak to me either, when finally he answers in a very low voice, pretending not to speak at all.

"I cannot talk to you. Get away from me."

I try again, but this time neither Ishmael nor Queequeg says a word. They simply ignore my presence, as if I am but a breeze or a rope they've seen a million times. All the other sailors follow suit, and I quit trying and sit back against the railing, my face turned towards the sun.

I listen to the motorboats' loud engines as they pull the *Pequod* forward through the flat sea. When we reach the port the crew leaves the boat in haste, but to my surprise nobody tries to stop me from stepping ashore. I move quickly away from the ship, in case they decide to change their mind, away from the harbor, and only under the cover of the first row of houses do I stop to look behind me. I am curious to see what will happen and I squeeze in under a small wooden porch, and through the partition I soon spy legs trotting by on the cobbled stones. When Ahab finally wobbles past I sneak out and follow him through the village, back to the house. I let him enter and listen carefully by the front door before I make a move. By the sounds of it he seems to be rummaging around in the kitchen, and just as I am about to open the door and mouse inside, I feel wetness against my already wet feet. There's water flooding the streets.

The water pours quickly through the runnels that surround each cobblestone, but within a minute the channels merge, and in no time all the cobblestones are submerged. *What on earth is going on?* I watch the spectacle and before I regain my wits the water is well up my calves. At this point

I don't care if Ahab sees me, I just want to get out of here. I open the door and water wells into the house with such great force it's impossible to push it shut. I bolt for the stairs, ascending it in great leaps. Back in the room I hurry over to the window, my feet kissing the floor with every step, and I am amazed by what meets my eye. The water is swelling up the side of the house at what looks like an inch per second. I decide to leave it all behind, and flee into the closet. And it's there, between the rows of salt-crusted coats, that a siren begins a wailing cry in the distance. At the exact same moment, as if it was the siren itself that caused it, water rushes in under the gap along the floor. I waste not another second. I jump into the tunnel and slam the door shut against the flood, and start running, feeling that the whole mess is peculiarly familiar.

12

I know something is wrong as soon as I open the door back to New York City. Buk is there, standing on the corner outside the Palace, smoking a cigarette with an anxious look upon his face. When he sees me he flicks it from his lips and steps into the street without looking either way. He reeks of old beer, and the stubble on his face is longer and thicker than I have seen it before.

"Hey, kid, I was worried about you."

There's something disquieting about the situation and Buk's appearance that I can't put my finger on. He puts his arm around my shoulder, and as I let myself be pulled across the street I recognize it in his eyes. He is scared.

We don't go through the regular entrance, but instead continue south, along the Palace's side wall, for about half a block. We stop in front of a door that melds so thoroughly into the wall you'd have to know about it to see it. Buk knocks out a short rhythm with his hairy knuckles, and the door swings open.

"Thanks, Mitch," Buk mutters and pushes me in before he himself follows close behind.

"What's with all this?" I turn and ask, but he only puts a finger to his lips and nods for me to keep going. We walk through what must be the Palace's service corridor, where the light is dimmed and filtered into a pale emergency-red glow. It feels like walking through a submarine in distress; my hands, Buk's face, the walls, everything is red, but whenever I turn to ask what's going on, Buk puts his finger up and inclines his head to encourage me deeper into the passage.

The red-lit corridor winds through countless twists and turns before Buk finally stops me in front of yet another door. He leans forward, sets his red ear against it, and for a moment neither of us even breathes. Then, as if deciding it was all just a game after all, Buk straightens out and declares with a loud voice, "All right! Coast is clear, soldier!"

We come into a bar I haven't seen before, arriving behind the counter. The bartender turns to face us – his eyes are white all the way through – though blind, they still stare me down. I hurry after Buk.

"What's going on?" I lean across the table so he can hear my whisper. It's really superfluous, because music is drowning out conversations from every other table, but somehow whispering seems appropriate.

"They are looking for you. What the hell happened?"

I'm embarrassed, and unsure whether I should tell him what happened or not.

"I...I fell from the boat and..."

"It doesn't matter." Buk waves away my explanation with his hand. "What's important is that they don't find you."

"Who?" I say, expecting anything.

"The board, dummy. The Board of Librarians."

My head is spinning, and the music doesn't help one bit. It's a repetitive tune without words that loops through the same beats over and over. I shake my head like a wet dog to clear it out of my ears.

"Buk, I don't get it. Who's looking for me?"

"Do I have to spell it out for you? You ruined *Moby Dick,* and now the librarians are after you."

I want to stop right there to try and grasp the meaning of Buk's words, but he keeps going.

"They aren't really librarians – not in the sense that you would know them anyway, that's just what we call them. They are shopkeepers of this store of tales, the captains of these fantasy voyages, the banana republic militia, and they will come down upon thee with the wrath of a thousand howler monkeys if they ever catch you. Got that, kid? And I can't help you if they do. So from now on you have only one thing to keep in mind: don't get caught."

Buk keeps talking, but I am no longer listening. I hardly even notice the blind bartender delivering drinks to our table. I look at the contours of his back as he leaves and I interrupt Buk's continuous stream of words.

"You said the books were going to be all right again – you said that the next day everything would be back to normal. You said everything would be ok. And how is it possible that they have powerboats in *Moby Dick*?"

Buk smiles at me, or possibly at all the glasses on the table, but he does smile.

"Let me tell you something about women," he says. "They couldn't care less."

I sense more words on the way and, knowing the beginning of a ramble when I hear one, I just sigh and keep my mouth shut.

"It's only when the blade falls and we are sitting out on a piece of cardboard that they say, 'But I thought you knew what you were doing?' Baby, it seems you are out on that piece of cardboard."

"For chrissakes! Can you just tell me what is going on?"

I bang my hand hard on the table, so hard that the bartender hears it through the music and turns our way, and it works. Buk becomes serious.

"It's all right, Willy," he says to the bartender, who goes back to wiping the bar with an old rag, showing no more emotion than a zombie.

"The librarians are a group of tight-assed bureaucrats who want everything to stay the way things are. They don't care much for you running around in their stories, messing things up."

"Is that who Koob works for?"

"Koob? Who the fuck is Koob? Never mind. Listen, from now on we do things differently. We have to be more careful, that's all. You are safe here, and when the time is right we'll use the back door and continue with the list. Just stick with me and you'll be fine."

Buk must have sensed my hesitation, for he adds.

"You do want to get out of here, right?"

I silently nod, for what other choice do I have?

I spend the night in a very narrow room behind the bar. It is merely the width of a bed, and in it shines that same red light so prevalent in the corridor. But it doesn't bother me. On the contrary, I feel completely safe in it and sleep like a baby.

In the morning Buk pops his head in to wake me, but I am already up.

"Ten minutes" is all he says, like a general notifying a soldier of mission ETD, and I try not to think about anything while I dress, except getting through the list so I can go home.

I let my subject go on ahead and follow at a safe distance. *If anything, I am at least getting good at tailing people*, I think. I catch his head as it disappears through the closing door, but just as I'm about to lay my hand on the handle I feel one on my shoulder.

Apparently my sneaking isn't as smooth as I thought it was, an assumption that is confirmed by the man attached to the hand.

With a slender and bony frame, a pointy face drawn long and thin into a snout, and hair sticking from his nose like whiskers, the man looks like a cross between a bird and a well-groomed rat. His name, which he is quick to offer, is Doc Daneeka. It does ring a bell.

I'm not sure why, but when he presents his hand to me, as if we were at a bistro or a business meeting, not in a murky tunnel under Central Park, I shake it without thinking.

"Buk said I'd had to hurry to catch you, and he wasn't kidding."

"What do you want?" Something about his appearance rouses my suspicion.

"Good, cutting to the chase. I like that. Buk said you were a smart kid."

"Tell me what you want." I press on, not in the mood for games.

The man called Doc Daneeka blinks a few times, and swallows, then gets to the point. "I want you to be me."

"Excuse me?"

"I want you to be me, Doc Daneeka. In there," he adds and looks at the closed door.

"How...what do you mean?" I'm confused.

"You take my clothes" – he begins unbuttoning his khaki shirt – "and you go in there pretending to be me. It's the safest way."

Finally I understand. It is all part of Buk's new plan to keep me out of trouble. Take one character out, put in a replacement. Boom, no easy-to-spot extras hanging around set. If it wasn't for one thing it might have been a good idea.

"That will never work," I say "I don't look even the slightest bit like you."

Doc smiles, but somehow it has the opposite effect; he only manages to look sad.

"Trust me, in there it won't matter. You just find the tent with the chair outside, stick with the version that you are me, no matter what, and everything will be just fine."

There is really nothing more to say. If Buk thinks this is the way to do it, then so be it.

Doc and I exchange clothes, and who would have guessed it, we are almost the exact same size. When we are done I look down at myself; I feel ridiculous. Khaki this and khaki that, I am a helmet short of an expedition. But I realize there is no use complaining.

"I've already been in one war," I mumble, "I hope this one is shorter."

"Just remember, no matter what, you are me!"

Doc wheezes the last sentence after me as I duck through the gates to fantasyland.

It's warm and sunny on the other side. Well, technically, I am still inside, but the door opens up into a storage room that opens up into a kitchen, and as soon as I walk through it I find myself standing under a radiating sun.

I am on an island, somewhere in the Mediterranean, and I don't have to walk many steps from the mess hall before a sign fills in the blanks. Camp Pianosa. In the distance I hear the humming drone of airplane engines, but when I search the sky I can't spot them. It's a milky blue sky that spans the top half of the world, meeting the ocean, dark, wet, and placid, at the far end of camp and massive-bodied mountains at the other. I figure the airfield can't be far away, and I start walking, around the mess, towards a group of tents in the distance. I cross a ditch shielding a pipe, and beyond the ditch the tents rise from the ground in stately order. Each one has its own invisible boundary – I'd call it a garden, had the tents been houses, but now, each sun-bleached canvas sits on a simple dirt square that looks to have been trampled by a horde of elephants. I look for the splotched grey tent with a chair outside, just like the Doc described, and it isn't long until I find it.

Doc's tent looks like all the rest: standard military issue, a miniature big top for a down-and-out circus. I peel the tent flap to the side with one finger and cast an eye inside. From what I can see it's uninhabited, and I step through with a quiet "'allo," just in case. Alarmed by my voice, or my intrusion, a man on a bunk stirs and sits up swiftly. He rubs his eyes and blinks in my direction, trying to cut through the dusky light, and first when he spots me does the tension drop from his shoulders.

"Oh, it's you. I thought it was an oil company geologist again."

I say nothing, and after a few raspy breaths he continues.

"You know, if you'd have any brains you'd grab a shovel and start digging. Right here in the tent. You'd strike oil in no time."

I'm not sure how Doc Daneeka and the man are acquainted, but the Doc had said to just be him, so I choose a voice I gather is a few steps away from mine, but not too many, and go for it.

"Well, I might just do that as soon as this war is over."

"If this war is ever over we'll be sent home, dead or alive, and we will have lost no matter if we win."

With that the man stands up, on shaky legs, I notice, despite his otherwise impressive physique. He takes one wobbling step forward, then stands in the ring of light cast through the opening around the tent pole above, and at last can I study his appearance. I see a handsome Indian with a hard-boned face and silky smooth, black hair. He stands in the beam of light like a dark Jesus, and such is his agerasia, a divine revelation, that I for a moment forget to disguise my voice.

"What's your name?" I ask.

The Indian starts at my words and is suddenly wide awake, even the wobble seizes. He looks at me with darksome eyes that have now become wary and suspicious.

"You. Who are you?"

I swallow once, desperately trying to repair my foolish mistake.

"What I mean is, how did you sleep?"

The Indian still looks me over, but I sense that a flake has been chipped from his stone-cold gaze.

"Step forward, please," he commands, holding his hand open to the side.

There's no room for error, I remind myself as I step forward and feel the beam of light strike my face.

"Now, who are you?"

I answer him calmly.

"Why, have you lost your mind? I am Doc Daneeka."

The Indian keeps his eyes on me, but I am now quite certain that I can convince him.

"Hmm, I remember you differently."

"Well, things change."

"From last night?"

"Perhaps you forget easily."

"You don't look at all like the Doc."

"But I am the Doc."

"No, you are not."

"Yes, I am! I really am," I add with great conviction, and at that the Indian's construction of what the Doc looks like, crumbles.

"I thought it was you," he says, a smile now upon his lips. "Come, let's go outside," and he takes a step towards me so I have to take one equally long backwards, then another, and another, until we both stand on the dirt outside the tent. The Indian grabs me gently around my shoulders – I feel the great strength in his hands – and with his face close to mine, riding on a breath of stale liquor, he delivers his request.

"Let's start this day with some Indian wrestling."
I feel his hands come alive on my shoulders. They turn into hot steel pipes against my skin, smooth yet unbreakable, and I take a deep breath and prepare to be brutally slammed to the ground. Only at the last moment does an angel step forth to save me; a voice sounds from the heavens, and the Indian's hands miraculously return to human flesh.

"Doc! I'm so glad I found you!"

I don't know what Yossarian looks like, so I can't explain how I know that the medium-built man with black hair, black brows, black stubble prickled across his cheeks, and eyes so alive they look to be an accidental mix-up of parts – had he been a doll – is indeed Yossarian, and with his voice alone he saves me from the dreadful Indian wrestling.

"Doc, I don't know how to tell you this."

I duck out from under the large man's now completely cold and loose hands, noticing the disappointment in his face, and I turn to Yossarian.

"Might as well go back to bed," the Indian mutters. "If this war continues, we're going to need all the oil we can lay my back on."

Yossarian has stopped in front of me, displaying an earnest face without a single wrinkle. His brows run on an uneven angle, framing his eyes in a puppy-dog fashion that I gather must work wonders in certain bars.

"Doc, I think I'm going crazy..."

The moment the words leave his mouth a ripple moves through his body, and, just like the Indian when he first saw me, he freezes. His arms don't hang but stand out to the sides, as if holding an invisible box.

"You…who are you? Where's Doc Daneeka?"

The tone of Yossarian's voice is one of genuine concern.

"Don't tell me the Doc is dead, shot down over enemy territory? He always said he hated flying. Or worse, that they sent him home, or even worse, that he went crazy and grounded himself?" Yossarian winces.

But this time I am prepared, my voice, my posture, the sincerity, the whole kit.

"I am Doc Daneeka, and I'm just fine, thank you."

Yossarian looks at me quizzically, the wrinkle-free face struggling to create even the slightest fold. Even quicker than the Indian does he break down, and he shrugs his shoulders as if at least pretending to accept this obviously ludicrous claim, and gives up without a fight.

"All right, Doc. Well, I'm glad I found you. You see, I have important news. I've gone crazy."

I can't remember the dialogue by heart, I only know there is something absurdly illogical about it.

"So you say," I respond, and will forth my most earnest impersonation of a doctor. Leaning forward, I pretend to examine something in Yossarian's face; I stare into the whites of his eyes, and when I find what I am looking for I am pleased, but of course not surprised.

"Aha, looks like it."

"So, you mean…"

"Yup, you're crazy all right."

As soon as I say it, Yossarian really starts acting crazy. He hyperventilates and rolls his eyes around in big circles inside their sockets. It's as if he wants to say something but first has to figure out how to say it. Finally he squeezes it out.

"Ehm, isn't there a rule that says you have to ground anyone who's crazy?"

"I don't know, but that sounds fair to me. Or maybe it should be the other way around? I mean, if you are crazy, you don't really care about anything real that happens in the world, right?"

Yossarian doesn't appear to have heard a thing I said, and continues, reading his lines from some internal script.

"Then why don't you ground me? I'm crazy. Ask Clevinger."

"Oh, I believe you," and I add, for effect, "son."

"But…"

"But what?" I say, feeling slightly irritated, for I remember clearly that this is all Yossarian ever wanted.

"But… even though I tell you I'm crazy, and ask to be grounded, you still believe me?"

"Sure, I'd be crazy not to, right?"

"Right, right. So, you are saying…?"

"Yes, that's exactly what I am saying! You are grounded!"

Maybe it's because I expected, if not dancing and wild laughter, at least some form of joyful expression, that Yossarian's reaction puzzles me. All I get is a glare of suspicious uncertainty.

"But, isn't there a catch?"

"A catch?" I pretend not to know, although I know exactly what catch he is referring to.

"Well, that the fear of danger is the process of a rational mind, and you'd have to be crazy to put yourself in that position. But once you ask to be let off the hook for reason of that same fear, you are considered sane and have to fly more missions. You remember, don't you?"

It is really getting on my nerves, the way Yossarian argues against his own point.

"Listen, buddy, do you want to be grounded or not? 'Cause you sure are acting crazy enough."

"No, no, I'm crazy, I'm crazy!"

"Fine, then it's settled once and for all. You're grounded," I say and turn around, stepping back into the tent.

The Indian is sound asleep in his bunk – the days seem to move quickly on the other side – and seeing him there makes me sleepy too. I resist an urge to just throw my weary body down on my bunk, and I settle for gently leaning back and closing my eyes.

But I don't get many seconds of peace. An annoying whisper calls for me from outside the tent. "Doc, doc. Are you there?" it hisses, time and again. I try ignoring it, but it is a persistent call, and finally the disturbance becomes greater than the comfort of keeping my eyes closed.

"What is it?" I spit out before I have even flung open the tent flap, assuming that it is Yossarian again, back with another silly argument for why he is, or isn't, crazy. Instead an unfamiliar face looks at me and I at it, and then it speaks.

"Is Doc around?"

The man is short and chubby and wears the sort of glasses that no doubt earned him a top-seeded ranking in the bullies' league back in school.

"I am Doc Daneeka," I say unable to suppress a yawn.

"No, you are not Doc Daneeka," the chubby man states. "I know what the Doc looks like, and you don't look a bit like him." He tries to glance around me and into the tent.

"Trust me, I know who I am, and I am me, Doc Daneeka. Who else would I be?"

I speak with great faith and conviction, and although not totally convinced, the chubby man seems able to look past that in favor of his errand.

"Okay, then if you are the doc, Doc, can I be grounded? I feel very strange, you could almost call it crazy, and..."

"Sure. I don't see why not," I say and pat the chubby man once on his shoulder dubbing him, not into knighthood, but rather insanity.

Back on my bunk – I am halfway to dreamland – when I'm disturbed yet again. There's a tap on my shoulder.

"Doc, Doc, wake up."

I open my eyes and find a pubescent example of a man kneeling next to my bed, and he looks so embarrassed and nervous that his painful expression instantly blows away all my irritation.

"Wait a minute," the man begins, but this time I am faster.

"Yes, I am Doc Daneeka, really, and you are crazy for not realizing it and therefore grounded. No more missions for you, young man, and that's final."

The man-boy rises to his feet. Hardly a hair has sprouted on his cheeks, which are an apple-blossom blush of red. He doesn't speak, he only presses both his hands around my one outstretched hand, and for a moment I think he is about to cry. I use his grip to pull myself out of bed.

"Thank you, thank you, thank you," he repeats, and I walk with him to the tent opening.

"There, now hop along. You are free little bird," I say and push him the last inch outside, and before another soldier can storm my bastion of peace, I tie the flap down and secure it with a double knot. On my way back to bed I hear the boy's cry in the distance.

"He grounded me too! I am crazy and he grounded me too!"

Thankfully, the rest of the night is peaceful and I sleep like a child, although I dream that the trampled ground outside the tent is trampled again by countless crazy men in khaki uniforms, all here to see me about a diagnosis.

When I wake up the air is very still; not even the slightest breeze puffs from the sleeping body of the earth. I bask in it, let it hold me in its gentle hand, while I try to count the thousands of stars that spread out above me. Mother Nature in her ultimate display of vastness. It's too dark to make out much else; patches of black of various depths lie each upon the other, clusters of trees, the distant mountains. *Stars.* Still reclined, I turn my head and look around; it's all gone. The tent – the second bed, along with the Indian and everything else – it's gone.

I sit up and put my feet on the ground. Bare dirt, cool and slightly damp, touches the bottoms of my naked feet. *Naked feet,* I think, and I feel the sand sift between my toes. Where are my boots? I'm still wearing the khaki uniform, but where are my boots? And the tent? And, of course, the Indian?

I spend the night on my bunk, unmoving, my feet tucked in under me to keep them warm. *Indian style,* I think, but I keep from smiling. All I do is follow the night's movement towards morning. I spend hours looking at the stars, meditating in the moment until the waking sun comes to chase them away completely. Half asleep, half awake, I think about nothing. There's not a sound except nature's own interjections, and even those are infrequent and courteously quiet. There is only me and the void, and exactly that, the void, is what develops on the celluloid of dawn as darkness melts away. There's nothing to fill the picture – only a canyon.

Not even ten feet from where I sit opens a gorge so wide that a dozen Evel Knievels couldn't have jumped it. I can't even see the bottom. I can only guess that it's many hundreds of feet deep. In the middle of the span, circling on the sun's first warm winds, is a lone eagle. I don't know what to think; it's surreal, breathtaking, but surreal. The eagle cries out. It's a series of high-pitched whistles that sound more like the shriek of a seagull. Seagulls. *Moby Dick* pokes at my membrane.

It seems wasteful to leave the beauty of this place so quickly, but I don't want to take any chances. I force myself to part from the view and begin walking back in the direction of the mess hall. After only a few steps it strikes me: What if the mess hall is gone too, just like the field of tents? What if a canyon is cutting through that very spot? Panic stabs at my chest.

I jump the ditch with the pipe and continue running. My foot hurts from landing on a pinecone, but I don't let it slow me down. I press on, and when I round a cluster of trees there is a joyous moment as I find the mess hall within sight. *Everything is going to be okay*. I let the panic go with a deep breath, and just the act of relaxing my body's tension sets off a loud rumbling in my stomach. *As soon as I get back I have to eat something,* I think to myself and smile. But my smile quickly falls to the ground and shatters to pieces as another belch, this one louder, echoes behind me.

I spot it immediately. Dust rises in the distance, an odd wall of dirt cutting through the landscape, straight as a ruler. There's no wind, and it simply hangs there, a see-through curtain of pulverized rock. A faint crack whips through the air, followed by another aggressive rumble, and when the entire length of the dust curtain suddenly jumps one step closer, I understand what is happening: the canyon is growing. The ground is being eaten up by the hungry gorge one mouthful at the time.

For a moment I am able only to watch as the dust curtain jumps closer and closer, the rumbling a continuous roar in the background. Not until I feel the ground tremble so much that it tickles my naked toes, do I snap out of my vegetative state. I spin around, and start running for my life.

Twigs and pinecones cut into my pounding feet, but there's no pain; I just lock my eyes on the mess hall and pump my legs and arms as hard as I can. I fly across the dirt – contrary to what I fear, my running isn't the dream-running where the world moves as if stuck in fudge, and I pour down the path and reach the mess hall in a flash. I know the canyon is close behind, the relentless rumbling keeping pace with my every step, and without slowing I round the corner, catching a glimpse of the galloping dust cloud.

I tackle the door with my shoulder and fall headlong into the kitchen. I bounce back up, and as I dash for the storage room I can't help but notice the smell of fried bacon and eggs and baked beans, and this smell, which brings me back to Sunday mornings, is almost an insult in the face of the oncoming catastrophe. I kick it out of my head as I kick in the storage-room door. The safety of the tunnel is now only one step away, the loud rumbling right outside, and through it I hear a weak voice bleat.

"Help…"

I turn around and see him right away. Under the counter, squeezed in between the stove and a sink, is a man in a khaki uniform, scared half to death.

"Help…," he repeats meekly when our eyes meet. It's not even a real "Help!" with exclamation points, it's simply *Help…* followed by three periods, as if he wasn't sure *help* is what he really meant.

I don't think. I run back into the kitchen, grab the man by his shirt collar, and in one panic-fueled effort yank him up and pull him with me into the storage room. The rumble is now literally on the other side of the wall, the floor tipping towards one side, pots and pans falling from the shelves. *This is not real*, I think as I throw myself and my salvaged cargo into the tunnel and slam the door shut behind us.

My body rests flat up against the closed door. Through it the rumble is very faint, and when it finally dies out I turn to the man and look at him with interest. He lies collapsed in a fetal position on the wet tunnel floor, with his back towards me.

"Hey, are you all right?" I ask, still panting wildly.

My words roll away through the silence of the tunnel, echoing unhindered down the stone path. The man doesn't make a sound, not even a moan. I think he might be in shock, so I lean forward and put a gentle hand on his back and repeat my question.

"Are you okay?"

There's an explosion of movement as the man worms around, and between the moment when his face appears and his fist hits the side of my head, I both register and process his identity. It's Yossarian.

"You son of a bitch!" he screams, his words missiles shooting down the tunnel.

For a moment I am blinded – there's no pain, only darkness – and I brace myself for another blow. But there isn't one. Instead I hear weeping, and when my eyes stop watering, through the haze I see Yossarian leaning against the tunnel wall, his face buried deep in his arms.

"You son of a bitch," he sobs, and this time the words linger in the silence.

13

Yossarian follows me through the tunnel. With every other step he sobs, but he doesn't say anything, he doesn't even swear. It's as if he's decided, like an angry child, never to speak to me again. I can only guess that he is upset because I ruined his set, but hey, welcome to reality, Yossarian. Your world was imaginary anyway. Tomorrow everything will be back up and running again.

Buk is waiting on the corner, and this is where the soldier and I part ways. Yossarian crosses the street and turns left towards the main entrance without a word, while Buk and I head south, down the street, to the side door and the red-lit corridor.

The procedure is very much the same as the last, except this time we don't go to the bar. Buk takes me straight to my room and leaves me there.

"You must be tired, but if you need one you know where the bar is." And he points across the hall.

I want to tell him about the canyon and the almost total destruction of Pianosa, but I let it be. I'm afraid I will only make him upset again. Besides, I feel awfully tired.

"Pick you up tomorrow, kid."

Left to myself, it isn't long until I fall asleep. Perhaps it's the solitude that brings it on, perhaps it's the red light. Either way,

I lie down on the bed that just about fits in my small corner of a pretend world, and I am immediately rocked to sleep.

I sleep well, despite by dreams. I should really say *dream,* for it is only the one that stubbornly repeats itself. It begins with me waking up – not in any real sense, it only happens in the dream – and I am not in the red room anymore. I am on the floor, on a mattress laid down before a fireplace. It's an old fireplace, cold and unused. One can tell that it came with the building, that it one day was a fireplace, but then it was cleaned out and painted the same color as the wall, perhaps even corked shut. The second thing I see are books: they are stacked in the cranny that once held burning logs.

I get up, and when I look around I notice more books. They cover the walls completely, as if there were no walls at all, only books piled in the shape of a room. But then I see a door in the midst of them, a green-painted door, and all of a sudden I can see the shine of a whitewashed wall between the books, here and there.

It is not my library. Under other circumstances I might have been led to believe it was, for there is a desk, on an angle similar to that of mine, and there is the fireplace, and a mattress on the floor, but there the likenesses end. Not counting the books, of course.

First of all, there are no windows in this room. And the layout is much different – the two long walls and the two short ones meet at different angles – I am quite sure of it. And the air – in the dream the room smells of something particular, something that isn't old glue or paper or even grease stains, but something else. Something clean.

Nothing much happens in the dream, I simply walk through the room, the library that isn't really a library. The dream begins and ends the same way; I lie down on the mattress to take a nap, and the moment I close my eyes I wake up in the red room.

There's nothing scary about it, quite the opposite. I feel safe there. It's the repetition that worries me. I know it means something, the room, the fireplace, the books, but I can't for the world figure it out.

Buk is there as promised in the morning. I don't know why he insists on taking me; maybe he needs a project to give him reason and direction. But not really, I decide.

"Hey, Buk," I say as we walk through the red corridor.

I feel like a man on a mission, an astronaut boarding the spaceship for yet another ride into the unknown. It's almost ceremonial.

"You know, that was nice and all, what you did with Doc Daneeka, but it isn't really necessary. I can take care of myself."

"Mmm," Buk says, and I think it's a strange reply. Does it mean that he thinks I can't, or that I can?

"And it was really a close call again, but this time it wasn't my fault."

"Don't worry, kid, it's all going according to my plan."

Another strange reply, I think, for, as I understand it, it is *my* plan, to get back to reality, not his. This, and the sort of arrogant air that I've noticed about him the last few days, and the way he meets me at the corner as if we were lovers or something, is beginning to annoy me. I no longer feel like doing him a favor every time I step inside a story. It should be the other way around. I am about to tell him how I feel as we near the subway service entrance, but I never get a chance, for Buk spots my mark.

"Go get 'em, kid!" and off I go, like a well-bred hunting dog.

I know at once that I've arrived in some fuddy-duddy British girly novel even before I happen to overhear Mr. Darcy's name, and it isn't long after that I realize exactly where I am. The ball at Netherfield.

I arrive through a door in the wine cellar, a heavy, ornate thing that only opens halfway before it stops against the back side of a wine shelf. Candlelight from the corridor outside flickers into the room, and I simply follow the oil lamps on the wall, which lead me up the stairs, through the servants' quarters, to the grand hall.

I should be well used to it by now, the sudden transition from one reality to another, but as I enter the ballroom I am still struck by the grandeur of it. The hall, no doubt constructed of stone like the rest of the building, is completely draped in fabric. Red velvet curtains hang along the walls from ceiling to floor, and glowing oil lamps, far more elegant than those in the cellar, protrude through almost unnoticeable cracks in the textile.

The floor is a well-polished, dark wood, though I can tell by the patina where carpets lay before the dancing floor was cleared.

Not even the ceiling betrays the room – it is covered with elaborate paintings, like the ones you'd see in a cathedral, and in the midst of it, crowning the entire room, hangs a gigantic chandelier.

Netherfield is a grand old estate, the kind of place that will cost a fortune to heat in a couple of hundred years, and I self-consciously wipe my feet before I enter the room.

I see ladies glide across the floor in exquisite, rustling dresses, revealing neither feet nor legs. I attract a few sideways glances, then a few more, and soon most all of the guests have eyed me – or rather, I realize, my most improper costume. I'm still wearing the khaki uniform that I borrowed from Doc Daneeka.

I must look like a toad amongst all the brightly colored cloth that shines in the flickering light. Like moving pastries, the ladies slip forward and sideways, and the men, all wearing the same outfit – a red, military-cut riding suit – stand around like rigid poles, ready to catch the moving pastries in case they should suddenly decide to twirl and drift too far.

I move quickly along the side of the hall and mix with a crowd gathered around a punch bowl. My attire draws more glances and not a few whispers, but when the music begins anew the stranger in the odd outfit is quickly, if not forgotten, then at least politely ignored.

I watch a few dances while entertaining myself with a number of glasses drawn from the punch bowl. I feel a bit lonely, even among the cluster of red coats and puffy dresses. Couples fill the dance floor, hand in hand, with straight backs and needle-point necks that, at their most daring, tip slightly to one side in an aristocratic greeting. Bodies keep a respectable distance from each other: there's not a crotch in the vicinity of another crotch in the entire room. A sexless dance by dolls with wooden groins, as I suspect Buk would have put it. I also suspect he would have approved of the punch bowl as much as he would have disapproved of the dance. Thinking of Buk here with me, staggering to stay upright, shouting foul things at his performing colleagues, I instantly regret any malicious thoughts I might have had about him. After all, the old bastard is only helping me get through my damned list.

I finish what's left in my glass, I forget which number; *To Buk,* I think, *bottoms up!*. Strengthened by the powerful brew, I decide to spice things up a bit. I stride over to a missus who happens to be standing nearby. Gallantly I bow to her while spinning my hand, just as I've seen in any number of movies from the era, and I grab her by the waist and pull her onto the dance floor.

Her protests are futile, the act of many detailed rehearsals, and perfectly suitable for the occasion. I listen to them with great pleasure for they only make her seem sweeter.

"You are too hasty, sir," she cries. "You forget that I have made no answer to your request. Every lady…"

"You forget, my lady, that I have made no request," I interrupt, immensely enjoying myself all of the sudden.

The music flows, and her tiny hands feel warm and a bit sticky in mine. She glances at me, both fearfully and with great curiosity, and I watch as roses bloom upon her cheeks while she does her best to keep composure.

"I dare say, I am not entirely fond of your manners, Mr…?"

"You can call me Al, bam ba ba ba," I sing back.

"Pardon me?"

"My name is Jonathan," I say and pull her so close to me that our bodies meet along the entire front. I can't say what's gotten into me, besides the punch, but I imagine Buk smiling from the sideline, at the sight of our happy crotches. However, the lady is far from smiling.

"Heavens, man!"

She pulls away from me, her blossoms now signaling an angry red. But I'm afraid the effects are wasted on me. I only find her slight wrath incredibly desirable and, seduced by the heat of the performance, I lean forward to kiss her. With a swift movement my lips fall upon her soft mouth, and just as swiftly a bolt from the blue strikes the side of my head. I've been smacked right across my ear, and the blow sets my head spinning.

There is some commotion in the dance hall, but I can't make out the details. From out of this unfocus I can only play along as a pair of steady hands grabs me by the shoulders. I'm not angry – on the contrary – I feel only a tremendous gratitude towards my anonymous helper, for his – it must be his – support in my state of disarray. That is, until he begins shaking me about like some rag doll.

With the violent shaking, on top of the spinning, on top of the many glasses of punch, I lose what little control I have left. I try to formulate some string of words that will hopefully cause the shaking to cease, but I succeed only in bringing forth a gargling stream of liquid with a force that surprises even myself. It works. With just the one quick spurt, both the spinning and the shaking end at once. Soon my eyes regain their ability to focus, and what they find before them when they do is a man I can only presume is Mr. Darcy.

With my bile dripping down his vest and jacket, his expression one of utter surprise, I am not the only one who sees a looming disaster about to move into the realm of reality.

"Oh, Mr. Darcy, please don't mind this filthy recluse!"

Mr. Darcy stares at me wildly with the blackest of eyes, and I quickly reverse the smile that has begun to crack open across my face. He is ready to strike me down, I am quite sure of it, but the moment he sees fear turn my face pale as a ghost's, he restrains himself with smug contempt before he can land even a single blow.

But it's not the threat of Mr. Darcy's fist in my face that frightens me. In fact, he could have held a gun to my head and it wouldn't have changed a thing. The reason I turn pale, the reason that makes me forget everything about the ball, the dance, the vomit and Mr. Darcy suddenly appears on the other side of the ballroom. There, through an open double door with a thick wooden frame, a huge lion pitter-patters in.

My first thought is that he has the most magnificent mane I've ever seen – it looks almost blow-dried, the way it stands out and bounces with each of the big cat's soundless steps. Within seconds screams are unleashed, and Mr. Darcy and everybody else who's had their eyes trained on me, turns around to find an intruder in their dance hall.

I don't know why the lion is here, which loophole it has arrived through, but it doesn't change the fact that it is. It looks our way, as if tasting the air, and I am so scared that I can't move a limb. Then, without warning, as is inevitable in a bad dream, it starts straight for us, and with but a few accelerating steps it is upon Mr. Darcy. As from afar I can only observe the lion's front paws, incredibly soft-looking mitts, rest on Mr. Darcy's shoulders, and from any other angle one could have taken it for a cuddly beast lovingly licking his master's face. Except the lion isn't licking Mr. Darcy's face, it's chewing on it. Crushing his skull inside its giant gape.

It might be my spew, the sour soup of semidigested foodstuff. The thought penetrates my mind as I feel the wetness of my own shirt, and with that I am finally able to breake loose. I turn and run. All around there are screams, and from the midst of them the guttural roar of the lion, which in turn produces even more screams. Fortunately, it seems interested in no one but Mr. Darcy, who he now tosses and shakes like a dolly manhandled by a pack of dogs.

I run, feeling the seconds pass in minutes, and I have no clear idea what I'm doing. I'm overcome by terror and only subconsciously do I aim for one of the windows. In midstep I pick up a cast-iron bull from a desk and fling it with great force against the glass. I turn around one last time and see that the lion is now dragging Mr. Darcy's bloody body around the room – attempting, one might say, a macabre dance with him – and I hurry to jump through the hole and into the night, without a thought for what is waiting below.

Luckily, the fall isn't great – I land on something soft and tumble forward and when I come to a stop I spring right back up and start running. Into the darkness across the lawn I go, away from the house and away from any lurking beasts, and only when I am wholly out of breath do I stop.

I see it in the distance; it is a lighthouse in the night, one exclusive island of honey gold floating in a wide sea of blackness. I catch my breath and watch it twinkle, and then I start running again. The light, it isn't just illuminated windows: it is flames licking the nighttime sky, and even from this distance I'm pretty sure I see a figure jump from a window and into the night.

I run until I am forced to slow to a trot, then a steady walk, then a tired stroll, and finally I stop moving all together. The view of the burning Netherfield is long gone, and the blackness of the night – it only grows so completely black in the countryside – surrounds me on all sides.

I must have traveled across a wide field, for the surface is everywhere soft and level with smooth grass, and even though the land gently rolls up and down I never once stumble. It isn't a very cold night, and the exercise has kept my body warm, but now that I have stopped I start to feel the chill.

I sense something large and ungainly moving in the darkness. I don't so much hear or see it as I feel the ground tremble. In all likelihood it's just a cow, but in case it isn't – the image of Mr. Darcy caught in the lion's jaws once again flashes before my eyes – I move quickly in the opposite direction. There I come about an island of trees and climb the first one that offers me thick enough branches, and I settle in a fork for the rest of the night.

I'm not conscious of falling asleep. The stars appear to sit a mere arm's length away, where they sparkle through the few sparse leaves above my head, and when I open my eyes with a jerk, there it is, a milky white sky.

It is more troublesome to get down than it was to get up. I have to hang on tightly by my hands and find a branch on which to place my feet, and when I finally drop the last bit to the ground my hands are cramping.

For a moment I think it is going to be a problem – which direction do I go to get back? But my worry turns out to be totally unwarranted. As I step through the trees I at once see the pillar of smoke rising on the horizon.

I begin working my way back. I compliment myself, for the lay of the land is just as I guessed the night before: gently rolling hills of green grass bulge from my nighttime perch to about where I must have first stopped to look back at the burning house. Here and there it is splotched with clusters of trees, so dense and lush they look impenetrable. Where the hills end a sort of flat field, kept clear of cow dung, forms a giant tongue that rolls all the way up to a low stone wall that marks the border of Netherfield Park.

The world is deserted, but I still move with great care. I make my way through the park and when I am finally close enough to see it I can't belive my eyes: there is not much left of her. What was only yesterday such a grandiose manor – it's a sight that amazes, how a stone house can be so totally devastated by fire – is now just a ruin. The roof has collapsed, along with most of the walls – the only wall still partly whole is one connected to the fireplace. It's charred completely black and stands naked and alone, taking a defiant stand against the sky.

I approach the smoldering remains cautiously, but there is no sign of life anywhere. Heat still radiates from the ashes, and I can only get so close before the air becomes too hot to breathe. I simply walk back and forth, in search of nothing, but on the lookout for anything, and when I become tired of walking I go once around the entire estate and it is there I find it, the next surprise. There's a trailer parked on the gravel in front of the once-dashing entrance.

The trailer, just like the lion, doesn't fit in. But the trailer, much unlike the lion, isn't a menace. And neither is the large flat-screen TV, the king-sized bed, or the chilled cans of beer in the fridge that I discover soon after entering. The trailer is simply a fortunately misplaced prop, and I am glad to have come across it. My affinity for sleeping in trees has but all expired, and it's not long before I am comfortably soothed to dreamland on the big mattress.

I awake to a knocking at the trailer door. Still groggy, I get out of bed as quietly as I can sending an empty beer can rolling across the floor with an untimely clatter. But the knocking persists. I sift through my options: I am in a strange place – if I'm lucky, the door back is buried under an enormous heap of rubble, and if I'm not, well... But whoever is knocking on my door, I am quite certain it isn't the lion, and I sure could use the extra set of hands to help me dig. I take a deep breath and wait for the next tap. There it is. I swing the door open and... nothing. All I see is the empty driveway. *Strange,* I think, and that's all I manage before something hard hits me between the eyes.

It doesn't really hurt, but it startles me to such a degree that I throw myself down on the floor. Another knock rattles the side of the trailer and I catch a glimpse of something bouncing off to the side. I crawl forward and carefully peek over the edge: it's a pinecone, and in the tree, about ten feet from the trailer, sits a monkey. The furry little sniper is flinging pinecone after pinecone at me, and when he realizes that I have spotted him he leers and shrieks with laughter, shaking his branch wildly.

With the monkey off my back, I work all day. The ruin has cooled off sufficiently for me to walk around in it, and I begin by calculating exactly where the stairs leading down to the wine cellar should be. I can determine this without great difficulty by retracing my steps from the ballroom, which I in turn locate by the location of the giant chandelier. Amazingly, it lies nearly unharmed in a heap of crumbled stone. I pull the smallest remaining pieces of Netherfield to the side, and by nightfall I have cleared quite an area around the larger objects.

The next morning the monkey again wakes me with his pinecones, and after indulging in breakfast from the over-stocked fridge, I go straight back to work. I use a massive wooden staff as a wedge and nudge larger stones to the side, inch by laborious inch. Some are extremely heavy, but I can see that I am making progress. My hands ache and pulsate when I get back to the trailer, but there's something about the hard manual labor that gives me great pleasure. After dark, tired and with sore muscles, it isn't long before I am asleep in my shiny new trailer.

The days pass in this manner for almost a week – breakfast, monkey, stones, sleep – before I finally catch a break. When the last big stone slides aside I have only to drag away the burned remains of a wooden beam before the opening to the stairwell reveals itself.

I chance upon a flashlight in the trailer and with it as my guiding torch I descend into the darkness. In the sharply cut beam of light I discover that down here things are not much changed; soot has collected on the floor, but other than that everything looks the same. Most importantly, the walls are still standing.

In the wine cellar, many bottles have exploded from the heat, and the floor is so sticky and dark with dried wine that it looks like the back of a butcher's shop. The mess makes me feel uneasy, the way it gleams ominously in the light, and I head straight for the door. It has swelled and warped – I have to use all my strength to pull it open, but I never doubt that I will. I have worked much too hard for it not to.

14

After this brush with eternity inside a British love story, one would think that my desire to visit yet another had been entirely obliterated. However, and surprisingly so, it is quite the opposite. Every story so far has challenged me in many ways, nearly killed me in some cases, and almost kept me for good in others, but after seeing Mr. Darcy being eaten by a lion and after days of rummaging through the hot rubble of Netherfield, something has changed in me. I've come to realize that my life before Koob sent me to my doom was nothing but a careful, almost frightened, repetition of an existence that was at best... uneventful. Books are the love of my life, and although I seek nothing but release from this literary prison, I have discovered a newfound determination to enjoy every minute of my confinement. I know I will be back in that cold library sooner or later, but until then I will do my best to suck out life's marrow. Now, for the first time in my life, I feel the excitement of being alive.

I greet Buk with a smile when I step out from the subway service entrance. Like a faithful dog he has waited – I can tell exactly where, for that part of the sidewalk is covered with cigarette butts – and before I tell him about the lion, and Mr. Darcy, and the fire, I assure him that I am ready to be sent off to the next book on the list.

I travel through the tunnel to Ramsdale, 342 Lawn Street to be exact, situated in the midst of the sleepy New England countryside. This is Lolitaville, the territory of the illustrious nymphet Lo, her mother Charlotte, and the, I suppose, in a way, terrible man whose steps I am now trailing, Humbert Humbert.

It is the beginning of time, Charlotte is alive and well, and her passionate feelings towards one Mr. Humbert is still a wet secret locked in her mind. I become the second lodger; there are protests in Humbert's eyes, but I persist, and Charlotte relents and gives me the maid's room. I retire there for a brief nap, and when I wake I feel it is about time for dinner. I saunter down the steps nurturing some hopes of a home-cooked meal.

Even though I now have a greater understanding of the effect my presence has on the other side of the subway service entrance, it is still a surprise to see how the stories react to my intrusions. Like a body injected with a virus, the story at once begins to form defensive cells around the uninvited guest. They divide and grow, multiplying rapidly in order to bring homeostasis back to their abode. When I reach the bottom of the stairs I spot the virus right away. In front of me, Dolores, Lo, Lolita – not one, The One, but dozens of this nubile creation – swarm the living room. I can hardly believe my eyes; each one seem to be an exact copy of the next, identical to the very last freckle. Just like the antelopes on the wall back at the Palace.

One is on her back on the sofa, reading a magazine, her bare legs dangling off the side; another stands before the radio with closed eyes, carefully bobbing back and forth; yet another is curled up into a ball on the floor. I spot thirteen of her total in the living room – each one with her own function to perform – and in the kitchen there are another five. And through the window I see a pretty collection of Humberts and Charlottes scattered across the lawn.

Through this rapid division – although I never manage to catch one at the precise moment it parts – by night the number of souls are so great that I have to elbow my way back up to my room.

I sleep very lightly, ready to wake at the slightest change in atmosphere, and in the early morning I glance out the window. The neighborhood is now a solid field of Lolitas, Humberts, and Charlottes packed sardine-tight, side by side, covering every inch of the ground as far as my eyes can reach.

The pounding of my heart and the sweat down my back settles so quickly I dare no longer call it panic, and, as always, a way out presents itself. I discover that I can travel quite easily over the solid carpet of bodies simply by stepping on their shoulders. Once out of the fully crammed house, I actually come to enjoy this strange trip, tip-toeing about their heads towards the train station at which I arrived through a door in the back. The figures moan as I weigh them down, and I try to be as gentle as possible, but despite my efforts the moans increase the further I go. After much balancing – I feel like a clumpsy ballerina – I eventually reach the closed door, and I must use all my strenght to pry it open against the crowd. It's a tight squeeze and when I finally stand inside the tunnel – there's no denying the fact, the moans really are increasing in both strength and frequency – I realize the moans have nothing to do with me. It's from the ever-increasing pressure as the mass of bodies keeps expanding.

Soon I am in another place completely, where children are also rulers of their own domain, but in a very different way than the sensually teasing Los.

I arrive in *Lord of the Flies* through a door in a hollow of rock about halfway up the mountainside. It is early morning; the dawn is only yet a pinkish flush, and all the sounds are still subdued. I find them shortly after, the pack of kids baked so brown in the sun I can't tell where their tans end and the dirt begins.

They look at me in silence, wide-eyed, before one of them coos, "A-a-a grown-up. Finally a grown-up."

Everyone gathers quickly; we sit in the assembly down by the beach, and whoever speaks has to hold the white conch. When the initial curiosity has melted away under the scorching sun – along with nearly half of me in a small river of my own perspiration – the one question everybody wants to ask is finally launched by a larger boy called Ralph. How did I get here?

I remember all too well how it was to be a boy playing in the forest. I'd been a Boy Scout once myself, and they all seemed to live their characters so truly and vividly that I hadn't the heart to tell them the truth. Instead I have to think on my feet, and what comes out, while not wholly appropriate, is, "I walked across the mountain."

This is the starting point of a terrific unrest, and soon all kids take off in a race up the mountainside, the bigger ones already far ahead, while the littluns struggle to at least not be the last one up. And just like that I am alone again.

The water looks inviting. I go for a short swim in the emerald-blue lagoon and dry off just by walking back to the assembly. Not a soul has returned. It seems odd to me, almost rude, that all of them would leave the moment I arrive, and, despite the pressing heat, I start making my way through the brush that stands dense as an old man's beard between the beach and the mountain.

I see no sign of anyone as I climb: there is only myself and the pinkish rock, chunks of which occasionally come loose and roll all the way down, disappearing at last into the scrub.

I pass the door to the tunnel, and when I look up at the remaining half of the mountain, I think I catch a glimpse of a foot moving just over the very top and out of view.

When I pull myself onto the last slab of stone, the floor on top of the world, and gaze over what I had assumed would be just another slope, this time going down until it hit the beach, and finally, the infinite ocean on the other side of the island, am I ever surprised. From the top of the mountain, which I and all others readers of *Lord of the Flies* have for ages believed to be the tip of a deserted island, I'm greeted by a view of a modern city with glistening skyscrapers and elevated tram tracks that mushroom from the ground not even an hour's march away.

There is no ocean, only land, and a sky that is crisscrossed by swarms of airplanes and helicopters. There's a movement on the rocky slope below: there they are, the children. Like an outstretched pearl necklace their little bodies drape the side of the mountain, working themselves down towards the greenery and the paved road that snakes through the foothills toward the city.

I don't follow them. Instead I head back down the mountain a second time, wait for the moon to rise and sit and watch it so long that I can see it even when I close my eyes. Once during the night I go back up, just to see if it was all a dream, for my mountainside is so still and quiet it might as well have been part of a deserted island. But the city is still there, now illuminated, buzzing with electricity and burning neon.

I come straight up on Larimer Street, among the old bums and beat cowboys, and I follow Sal Paradise to a swanky apartment he shares with one Roland Major. Soon the boys come by, Dean and Carlo and some other fellows too, and I mix in with the lot, small-talking about this and that, carrying my own weight. There are no questions I can't answer, perhaps because, by now, I too look like a wayfarer in my khaki outfit. Then, as the evening approaches, the strangeness begins.

It happens little by little, but the change is as sudden as it could ever be. And it includes everything, the view from the windows, the whole of the apartment and everybody in it.

In the span of a few hours every single color, even grey, black, or brown, turns more and more vivid, as if someone outside the world was dialing up the saturation. By midnight, stepping out of the bathroom, I find that the transformation is complete. It is no longer Jack Kerouac on the road in Denver, the human version: instead it has become *On the Road*, the animated feature.

Sal and Dean and all the others have by some magical turn of events transformed into cartoons of their former selves. Everyone has greatly accentuated features – Dean's big nose becomes a huge, black, fistlike thing that hangs from his face like a ripe fruit threatening to drop to the floor – and their otherwise human qualities, knees and hair, have all melted into smooth blots of colored ink. The apartment floor is a murmur of an even brownish sludge, and the walls have become soft and swampy, as though if you jumped into them you would only be bounced right back.

I walk into the street, and there I discover that it isn't just a local occurrence at the Major's apartment block: the entire city has turned into a Technicolor beast poured from the tip of some gigantic pen. I am the only real human left.

Apart from these mere details – for what is reality anyway but color and form? – it seems to be business as usual. Cars and trams swoosh by on streets that have all become rubbery and slick; Denver itself stands the same way Denver stood when I arrived this morning.

I spend the night, one as strange as they come, slinking around Looney-Tune town, trampling its black rubber arteries and screeching around corners until the painted sun rises and colors the already painted background with a different palette. Then it's time for me to go.

The oily gloom is so compact I hardly notice that I have left the tunnel, much less that I have arrived in Maycomb County. I'm in a house, I know that much from the way the floor creaks as I move, and this I do with the utmost care, trying my best to avoid banging into anything.

These first of movements in a new place are always laced with the same confusion – every sense is sharpened, my mind busily collecting data about the unknown. Well, the known unknown, but even that isn't always what you expect it to be. This time, despite my carefully executed movements, I do walk into something, and it sets off a chain reaction.

As I gently sneak my left foot forward, my big toe nudges something hard. I'm guessing it's a cabinet, and in my side-stepping it I instead strike my hip against a sharp edge on what I realize must be the real cabinet, and for a moment my knee buckles. To keep my balance I throw my arm out, grabbing at whatever I can find to keep me up. That something turns out to be a lamp, which falls to the floor with a deafening crash. Instantaneously I hear the soft trampling of feet and I know I'm revealed.

His voice is that of a little girl's, but before he speaks, as the shuffling quiets down and I know someone is standing by the edge of the room listening through the darkness, all I hear is the soft rasping of a breath that is constantly on the verge of breaking into a cough.

A light comes on – a floor lamp – casting a gentle, tube-shaped glow, strong enough for us both to finally see each other.

"Who...who are you?"

In a way his weak and frail voice is fitting for his body, for it too looks frail and weak. But considering the length and age of him – he must be in his late forties, even fifties – the childish voice makes a curious impression.

His complexion is completely white, even in the gloom, with the electric light reflecting off of it. There's no meat on his bones; his skin is sunken and yet somehow tightly wound across cheekbones and eye sockets, eyes that are covered in a wet mist, as if looking through a thin layer of milk. It's him, I realize, the man forever bound to his house. The infamous Boo Radley.

We don't speak. Every word I try to pull from him is a struggle, leaving him winded and out of breath. I tell him

I'm sorry for breaking his lamp, that I am a sleepwalker and that I can't explain how I got here, and even though it all sounds wholly unbelievable, Boo Radley accepts my words without protest.

I ask him to show me the way to the front door, but instead of leading me he simply follows a few steps behind, watching as I guess my way through the darkness. The brightness outside surprises me: it's full day, something I would never have guessed within the walls of Boo Radley's dwelling. It's while standing there on his stoop that I get the idea. I really don't know why, I suppose I want to do something for him. Not just for breaking his lamp, but for the shy helplessness he displays. I want to take him out of the house, show him that the world is not such a dangerous place after all. I want to liberate him from the shackles of darkness.

I say, "Boo, you know that none of this is real, right?" And I bang my hand on the doorframe.

"You ever been to the Palace? I'll take you there if you want. Just come out with me for a while."

Boo stares at me, his face and body still safely within the shadows, and I don't expect him to move. It's just something I want to tell him because I don't think anyone ever has. But after a few moments of wallowing in doubt, he blinks his eyes a few times and takes a careful step out on the porch.

It's a beautiful day, sunny and warm. The brightness is harsh, even for my eyes, and I can only imagine how it must be for poor old Boo. He has already changed: although squinting, all cautiousness has up and vanished, and now he moves with poise, walking beside me as if my few words was all it took to cut him completely loose.

We walk through the gates, turn right, and continue down the road. On the other side, by an old weathered tree, stand two children. The boy is around twelve, the girl, wearing overalls, a few years younger. They look at us with platter-sized eyes and half-opened mouths as we pass them and continue down the road, out through town.

We walk deep into the countryside, alongside cornfields leveled to the ground, where the remaining stubs have been burned to a bleak brown crisp. The town is since long far behind us when a swift motion to my right catches my attention. Simultaneously, a wild whirring, much like that of an electric turbine, settles from a high pitch to a soft humming, and for the first few seconds, my mind doesn't compute.

It's a bullet-shaped steel structure the size of a barn, and it's hovering a few feet above the corn stubble. I've never seen such a machine in my life. And I've sure never anticipated one in a cornfield in Maycomb County.

From out of nowhere a man crosses the field with large strides. He looks determined, like one who moves on tracks. The man is none other than Boo Radley himself. Part of me knows what is about to happen, and I have the feeling I ought to stop it. I just don't know how. The closer Boo Radley gets, the faster he walks, and I realize that nothing in this world can stop him from going up to the ship. All I can do is watch. Too numb to even call out I see a hatch magically opens in the silvery body. Without hesitating Boo sticks one leg into the dark hole, pulling in the other while folding his body to fit, and just like that he is gone. Swallowed up by the bullet.

When the hatch closes the wild whirring climbs again to its high pitch, and the enormously oversized bullet shoots into the sky. Once again, the cornfield is empty and the world is silent, and I begin counting the minutes I have left before I can go back.

My trips through the tunnels continue without interruption, and with each one I become better at noticing the details. Or maybe it's the details that notice me, I'm not sure. All I know is that when I first read *The Catcher in the Rye*, I'm pretty sure Holden wasn't a vampire.

I arrive in New York, at the Wicker Bar on 54th Street – incidentally only a few blocks from where I left, although in a completely different era. Right away I spot Holden. I stand on the outside, looking through the window to where he sits at a dark-wooded bar next to another young man.

I make it inside without drawing attention to myself and take a seat within hearing distance of the two. It's the same old phrases, delivered by the same snot-nosed, spoiled brat the entire world knows as Holden, with the exception that he is now flesh and blood, and but a few feet from me. I listen intently for any familiar lines, guessing each word before he says it, and that's why my spine tingles when the rhythm suddenly changes.

It's not just the rhythm, but from Holden's lips comes a tirade of dirty words, a gurgle of cussing and abuse, and before I have time to process the out-of-characterness, he explodes off his chair and dives onto the poor fellow next to him with a roar. Holden pins the man with what looks to be a vise-tight grip; the fellow shakes and rolls without moving

Holden's body an inch, his neck caught firmly between our protagonist's jaws.

As the poor bastard's feet begin to tremble uncontrollably, I quietly get up and sneak towards the exit. Outside, with one last glance through the window at my once-favorite teen-angst antihero, I turn and run. The image of Holden with blood smeared across his face, the vicious predator looking up from the unmoving body on the floor, plasters itself across my mind, and I sprint to find a safe hiding place for the remaining hours.

Such trips leave me puzzled and scared, but then there are trips that fill me with life and, usually, a good laugh, which is exactly what I get in *The Great Gatsby*.

I arrive through a door inside the pantry at Nick's West Egg bungalow on the night of the party at the great Jay Gatsby estate next door. I follow Nick, though this time, remembering the unnecessary attention I drew on account of my outfit in *Pride and Prejudice*, I dress accordingly in one of Nick's spare smoking jackets.

The party is extravagant and grand, as expected, with women wearing peacock feathers and glittery dresses, and I soon lose track of Nick in the general commotion of the fabulous shindig. I know for a fact, before the night is over, that he will partner up with Jordan and eventually run into Mr. Gatsby himself. But, as so many times before, events take a turn of their own.

I am speaking to a man with large, owl-eye glasses, whom I had found in the library, marveling at Gatsby's collection of books. As we talk about this and that, the way two strangers usually converse at a party, I realize that the noise level has changed abruptly.

When I entered the library, all was in order: elegant women, wearing the height of evening-gown fashion, and picture-perfect examples of decadent male aristocracy had converged in small flocks. But as I bid farewell to the owl-eyed man and return to the party, I almost choke on my champagne. Everyone is either completely or half naked, busily copulating wherever they happen to be.

I freeze where I stand, expecting at any moment something just as extraordinary as the arrival of another UFO, perhaps this time crashing through the walls of the Gatsby estate. But nothing of the sort happens; there is only the copulation, which continues without interruption.

I spot Nick over by a navel-high vase. He isn't wearing any pants between his shoes and his jacket, and involved with him in a carnal dance is the woman I can only presume is Jordan. She too is naked as a newborn, and her eyes glow with passion.

I feel rather out of place, being the only one still fully dressed, and decide to leave straight away. I do so out through the back, where I have to apologize to the chef and a maid for disturbing them in their amorous embrace.

I spend the night in Nick's house, all alone, for he doesn't come home before I leave in the morning. I can't say I blame him, what with the Gatsby orgy taking place just around the corner.

15

While not all stories prove quite as exciting as *The Great Gatsby*, I appreciate each for its own qualities and events, and I am making good progress with my list. I tick off *Ulysses, A Passage to India, Don Quixote, Crime and Punishment, Great Expectations, The Tin Drum, Under the Volcano*, and many more, and soon half of the titles on the list have black lines cutting through them.

Between every trip I spend at least one night in the red room, and every time I dream about the library without windows. The more I dream, the more detailed it becomes, as if with every dream I add pieces to it, pieces that are already part of me. The fact of the matter is that the dream is so frequent that my image of the real library has become muddled. I can no longer picture the room in which I sat writing, the one they cleared for me on the second floor, the one with windows on each side of the fireplace. Now my dream library slides in and covers my real memory, and even though I know I shouldn't doubt myself or let a dream twist my mind, I can't help but think that maybe, just maybe, that room didn't have any windows after all.

I am running full steam ahead, ready to leave again after another night's rest, when, for the first time, Buk isn't on the sidewalk to greet me. I wait for him on the corner, until I begin feeling silly for standing there all by myself when I could be cozily napping in my room. So I simply let myself in through the side door and walk alone down the red corridor.

Before I hit the sack, I feel the need to rinse the traveling dust from my throat. As so many times before I enter at the back of the bar to get myself some refreshments. The barman – although blind, his senses are out of this world – greets me with the same solemn nod as always, which means, *Take what you need,* and I am just about to leave when, from a storage room in the back, Buk's harsh voice reaches me through the door.

It makes me curious to hear him here. I sidle up to the door and quietly press my ear to it – smoke pours out from around the doorframe and trickles in thinly spun yarns towards the ceiling, and the acrid smell of tobacco is so strong that I have to clench my lips to suppress a cough. Buk isn't alone in there, I can hear two voices inside, but only Buk's is loud enough to hear.

"We are halfway there."

"They have no idea who is behind it. They are fumbling in the dark."

"They are gone forever. World's eradicated from the future."

"The last readers. The book is closing."

"The resistance will be strengthened."

"Destruction is creation, creation is freedom."

"Destruction is creation, creation is freedom!"

With Buk's words echoing in my head, instinctively I know. I don't know exactly *what* it is I know, or *how* I know it, I just *know* that I know. Cold sweat has formed on my back and I shiver under its sickly embrace. There's a sharp pain shooting from my lower lip – I don't mind it, that pain is fine – it's my heart that really hurts. It's all a nightmare. A bad dream. It must be! Blood drips down my chin and stains my pants with dark splotches. Can it be true? Have I been so duped that I haven't been able to see what was right in front of me? All those stories... all those people... gone forever. And I killed them!

It's anger that frees me from my paralysis. It bursts the floodgates of restraint, and I rip open the door. There, standing in the dense, white cloud of smoke with two fat cigars like loaves of bread in his mouth, I find Buk, a surprised expression on his face, and before him, shaped by the smoke, is the face I so well remember: Koob.

"The resistance, Jonathan, think of the resistance!"

The words are hurled after me as I run as fast as I can through the red corridor. It must be Buk, for new words follow until I burst through the door and into the street, shaking them there.

"We will never be free unless we free ourselves. The revolution…Jonathan… wait!"

Now everything happens quickly. I run up the street towards the park, aiming for the tunnel once more, but at the corner I change my mind and turn towards the main entrance and the café. Like a bull I charge through the lobby; I recognize everything – the carpet, the elevator to my left, the fabric covering the walls – but I run past it all and continue straight into the parlor. I am looking for him, the little one with the hat, the prince of boys, frantically grasping at anything. And for a moment I think I have found him, sitting by the counter, coolly slurping down a milkshake. We look at each other – our eyes meet and there is instant recognition. I know him from somewhere… There have been so many faces.

"Help me. I didn't know," I say. "Help me."

But by then it is too late. He has already pressed the button on the transponder I see wedged in his hand.

"You son of a bitch," Yossarian says, and then everything goes black.

When I come to, I am on a bench in a room I've never seen before. I gather it's some sort of holding room, for above one door a sign reads *Exit*, and above another a sign says *Enter*, and all along the wall stretches the bench. Except for it, the room is empty. My head tingles more than aches, but other than that I feel fine. I don't get much time to figure things out, because soon the Enter door swings open and, after waiting for something to happen, I realize someone is waiting for me to step inside.

Everything is surreal.

They say I am part of the Resistance.

"You are part of the Resistance!"

I stand below an elevated row of people of whom I can only see heads and upper torsos. The man in the very middle – he must be the leader, for he sits in the largest chair of all – is the one speaking down to me. He is balding and grey, not only his moth-eaten cardigan, but likewise his ashen skin. The eyes that glare critically at me from behind a pair of rounded reading glasses are the kind that would rather be looking at letters, specifically letters in combinations that satisfy – namely, words.

The Board of Librarians stare down at me, all with the same strict proofreader's eyes, and I can tell that they have detected a major typo before them. It's nearly comical how they all look alike; I can't remember ever seeing such a quantity of cardigans, conservative hairstyles, and overall mousy appearances together in one room, but I refrain from drawing my lips into a smile. Buk's words still ring fresh in my ears: "They will come down on you with the wrath of a thousand howler monkeys." Although I seriously doubt it, from the look of them – it seems to me the only way they can hurt me would be by slapping me with a late fee. But it's not hard to stay somber-faced as I listen to their accusations.

I've destroyed fifty-two classic works of fiction –

"You've destroyed fifty-two classic works of fiction"

– and killed or otherwise terminated thousands of characters –

"and killed or otherwise terminated thousands of characters"

– by disrupting, intervening, and changing the course of events –

"by disrupting, intervening, and changing the course of events"

– that eventually led to their collapse.

"that eventually led to their collapse."

I am stunned. I don't know what to say. These grave accusations imply that I, as part of the Resistance, have planned and then executed the events that later led to the destruction of said books.

"Resistance? You mean Buk?" I ask, and all the librarians begin to whisper among themselves.

"I just wanted to go home. Koob said I could go home, and so did Buk, if I only finished the list."This draws another wave of whispers.

But it is useless. They bring Yossarian to the stand, and with his tearful testimony that I, in the shape of Doc Daneeka, granted him permission to go home, thus overturning the entire plot and causing it to fall to pieces, the librarians are already convinced of my guilt. It doesn't even matter that I tell them how I am really one of them.

"I am really one of you! I'm a librarian!"

But they ignore me, and the nail in the coffin comes from Doc Daneeka himself. Apparently the two of them are the only survivors of my literary odyssey, and with his testimony about how Buk and I talked him into giving me his costume, as he calls it, the case is closed. Little does it help that I, in my desperation, shout from my position down below, "But this is ridiculous! It's all made up! None of this is even real!"

My outburst is like a lashing whip across the backs of the entire Board of Librarians; they all twitch and look at each other with resentful eyes, then shoot cold stares my way. I am nothing to them now.

The one on the taller chair lifts his wooden club over the pulpit and reads from thin air the verdict: I am to walk through that door – he points with the club towards a door at the end of the courtroom – where I am to be sentenced to travel on foot through the Land of Fantasy.

I don't belive what I hear. The Land of Fantasy? Then what is this? The Land of Reality?! But there is no discussion or chance for appeal, for as soon as the chief librarian drops his wooden club with a measly sort of bang, two guards come from out of nowhere, grab me by the arms, and drag me towards the door.

If there is one thing that I am beginning to tire of, it's doors. They're always there at the beginning of things, hiding the future, keeping worlds separated. But I don't have much choice and I walk into the blackness on the other side with a straight back.

It's not what I have expected. Not at all. I have only taken a few steps when, like little Alice, I fall through a rabbit hole.

It's only a few seconds long, the fall, but harrowing enough. I have plently of time to think that I'm not ready to die, and just as I realize that I ought to leave this world screaming, I land comfortably enough on something soft and bouncy.

I momentarily collect myself – I'm without either dents or bruises – before I pick myself up, and brush the dust off my clothes. After only a few steps I recognize that I've arrived in a queer place. A hobbit, a dwarf, a leprechaun, whatever you may call it, awaits me at the crossroads I inevitably reach, for there's only the one way I can go from the horseshoe-shaped chamber at the rabbit hole's end.

The little man – let's call him the evil dwarf, for with that face he can best be described as such – stands at the point where the path I am on forks into two separate directions. It rings a bell: I recognize the setting, the dwarf and the forking road, but before I can properly recall it, a voice from behind my back interrupts my train of thoughts.

"Jonathan? Is it really you?"

Despite having seen her up close only the one time, the day she came to my apartment, I have not forgotten her face.

And at this very moment, with so many question marks still to be erased, I only know one thing for certain: I love her with all my heart.

Johanna fills me in on what happened until the evil dwarf clears his throat with the resonance of a much larger man. What she told me was surprising, but nevertheless fit the puzzle perfectly.

She had come looking for me, first at my apartment, then at the library. At first Harry wouldn't let her see me – he'd said I needed peace. But when she persisted, Harry had mercy on her and showed her the way upstairs.

She had knocked on the door, and when there was no answer she had simply gone inside. She saw the desk, the mattress, and the fireplace, but nowhere was I to be found. Suddenly a voice called to her: "Johanna, Johanna," it said. It was a weak and feeble voice, and she scrambled to find its source. Soon she had it narrowed down: it was coming from the fireplace.

Had I crawled up into the chimney and gotten stuck there? Johanna leaned forward as far as she could and called out my name, "Jonathan?", and without knowing how, she stumbled forward – she said it felt as if she had been sucked down a drain – and after falling into darkness, she too landed in the horseshoe-shaped dead end behind us.

The evil dwarf rasps again, impatiently, as if he has more pressing things to do than stand in the middle of a crossroads all day, but I ignore him.

"I'll get us out of here," I say, "I promise."

I look into her eyes, but my assurances seem wasted. She doesn't appear at all to be worried. If anything, she seems more concerned about me.

"I've been worried about you. Are you okay?"

The evil dwarf harkles a third time.

"Let's get out of here," I say, this time somewhat grateful for the dwarf's interruption.

The dwarf spreads his arms and asks us to choose. One way leads to doom and destruction, the other towards salvation. We can ask anything we like, but we only have the one question. And one more thing, only every other time will his answer be truthful.

"What is your question?" The evil dwarf hisses.

A minute passes.

There's surprise in the evil dwarf's face as we leave him standing in the fork.

"How did you know?" I ask.

"Oh, don't you remember?" she says without a hint of pride.

Our conversation takes a detour. We skip past what I think are the most pressing questions, where we are and how to get out of here, and instead she begins telling me about her past.

She is an only child, the daughter of a man and a woman who – and this is the impression she gives me, but from which words I so presumptuously interpret it I can't say – were somehow nonexistent. Perhaps it is the way she uses the past tense when speaking of either of them, saying "my mother was" and "my father used to" and so on, but it might very well also be a thing of the subconscious. All in all, and hauntingly so, everything she tells me appears vaguely familiar.

She grew up fast in a Midwestern town; her mother was a hairdresser and her father a physicist at a big research facility that, if you asked him, at least as a little girl, you were told produced the plastic that was later molded into the mannequins in storefront windows all across the country.

The little girl grew taller and brighter, and one day she realized that the research, which in all honesty may also have involved some type of plastic, was mostly put to use for explosives. In a strange way this discovery fascinated her, that her father's creations fell from the sky a million miles away.

It wasn't long after this revelation that her father was sent to the funny farm. Those are the words she uses: the funny farm. She doesn't go into specifics, but I can tell she holds her father dear. There's tenderness in her voice when she tells me. He used to read to her, from when she was a little girl of five or six onwards, beyond when she could read well herself. It was simple. When the words fell from his lips "it made the story come alive."

Her mother stopped doing hair and, without a purpose or a husband, quickly succumbed to pills, daytime TV, and cigarettes, which eventually made her skin as light blue as the smoke that constantly filled the TV room.

When she passed, the house was put on the market quickly. Johanna could not stay there even one night, the liquid metallic scent having penetrated every part of the house, including the porch and the mailbox. She got a hotel room for the time after her mother's funeral.

Mimicking a diver, she took a big gulp of air outside and ducked into the house and didn't exhale until she was back on the doorstep again. Using this method she fetched the few things she wanted to keep. The rest was sold along with the house.

All in all she salvaged three things, all of which had belonged to her father. The three things were a painting, a book, and a statue, and that they too smelled of smoke was somehow bearable.

There was a bond between father and daughter that was never to be shared by her mother, and that was almost certainly a splinter in her mother's flesh for as long as she lived. But that's how life had wanted it, there was no one to blame.

The strings of her past all but severed, she moved around in a jumble. From city to city she roamed, state to state, like some bible-peddling saleswoman vagabond. She stopped nowhere long enough to attach either a pet or a boyfriend, packing and unpacking boxes with things that didn't really matter, but always bringing with her the three smoke-scented tokens.

She was only passing through when she came across me. But it wasn't a coincidence that she had walked across the lawn in the park in front of where I lived. She had, like everybody else, heard of the news of the history-making winner, the soon-to-be-writer of the last book in the world. Through a relative at the Social Security she had been able to track me down.

There is a *why* on my tongue, but it needn't ever be dropped, for she continues without it.

Every day she walked across the lawn in the park, feeling my eyes on her. She saw the black-coated men, but they suspected nothing, taking her for a simple passerby. She ached to get inside the old apartment building to meet me. And for what? Of course, it all went back to her father.

She remembers that they both cried after *Don Quixote*, not because it was a particularly sad story, but because the book had come to an end and would never again serve them that first reading pleasure.

When the books had all run out – this was before the paper shortage, what she meant was the stories – when they had all been read, at least the ones that mattered, her father did the only thing he could think of. He put pen to paper himself.

Propelled by the mighty force of his phenomenally intricate mind, he worked every night after he came home from the plant, for weeks on end. When she asked him how it went, and she did every morning, he answered with a secretive smile and always the same words: "It's coming along." It's coming along, just as the days so languidly sailed by, and she could hardly contain herself. Then, one day, it happened.

She remembers that day vividly. It stands out as one of her most precious childhood memories, in full Kodak color, surpassing even Santa and her first kiss behind the school gym, which was to come a few years later.

Fall had just arrived, actually that very day. The leaves went from a smooth green to a leathery yellow overnight. Shiny cars glided under the trees that still lined the streets of her neighborhood, and no matter what color the cars were, their hoods all seemed yellow with the reflection of the leaves.

When she came home from school her father was already there. Later in life she realized it was about here it started, the misfiring of his mind, but that day she felt her heart jitter when he met her as soon as she came through the door. There was a smile upon his face, and her eyes darted to his hands but couldn't find them. She could hear the clock on the kitchen wall very clearly through the silence. Finally, when seconds had turned into small bombs, he brought out from behind his back and presented her with the gift he'd so lovingly put together just for her.

It was bound by hand with thin strips of satin and covered in a soft, cream-colored fold of leather. At first the leather seemed empty, only a smooth surface, but when she accepted the gift and her fingers ran across the hide, she could feel it. She followed the slight indentions where her father had painstakingly stamped each letter into the leather, forming the nearly invisible words: *The Last Book in the World*.

The road we walk on, or rather, the countryside on each side of it, for nothing but countryside surrounds us, floats by without change. Although it looks real – the gravel and dirt surely is, and the grass on each side, and the air we breathe, and the blue sky also – it still gives the impression of being a waiting room of a landscape. A computer-generated scene in a video game that just goes on forever.

Her words keep the pace, and we move along the one-wagon-wide strip of hard-packed dirt cutting through the too-green greenery. The forested horizon constantly lingers where it is, never coming closer no matter how far we walk. Johanna tells me about the park, how she crossed it day after day in the hopes of getting a glimpse of me, when the world eventually *does* change. The road leads us into a fairground, and Johanna falls silent.

I tense up, mentally and physically preparing for any surprise that might spring from behind a tent or a merry-go-round – this is after all the Land of Fantasy. We walk by booths at which you can throw balls at bowling pins, tents hiding bearded ladies and crab-toed men, and wagons selling roasted nuts dipped in honey, and little by little we relax.

On the surface it looks like an ordinary fairground, but walking through the rows of tents and booths, it hits me: we are the only visitors. The people we don't come across, clusters of fun seekers that should stand evenly distributed around the attractions, eating cotton candy and wearing silly hats, they leave a gap in reality. The only life we stumble upon are the attendants hawking behind their podiums without acknowledging our existence. Not a hello or even a nod of the head. Yet they all seem to be here, along with the tents and the booths, for our benefit. I get the feeling that the whole fairground is just an extravagant set erected for our visit.

When we pass a blue tent with red and gold tassels edging its roof, a man swiftly but quietly appears from behind the fabric. He's got a friendly and inconspicuous face and with one hand he holds it open just wide enough for us to squeeze through, inviting us inside.

The interior of the tent is lit by a single lightbulb dangling, illusively, from empty space. The light creates a floating bubble that illuminates a table, and all around that bubble is darkness, and the sounds from outside are subdued into near nothingness. Behind the table a man sits motionless. He appears to be waiting, for something, or someone, and I study him as we move closer. He is dressed in the style of an old-fashioned bank teller: a white shirt, a black vest, glasses, and a short-brimmed cap, also black. The first man has snuck past us, unnoticed in the darkness, and he now appears by the table, his hand again outstretched, inviting us to sit. The moment our backs touch the seats, the teller begins.

"You have five bags of coins. Each contains an equal number of coins, but one of the bags contains false coins. False coins weigh eleven units apiece and real coins weigh ten units apiece."

He doesn't look up at us, our eyes never meet; he only watches the bags of coins before him.

"This is a scale. It's only good for one measurement, then it will cease to work."

He looks at the scale and holds it for a brief moment in his hands.

"You may open the bags and touch the coins as you please, but I can assure you there's no way of telling them apart."

Still without a glance at us, he pauses, sharpens his focus, and fires the question we know is coming.

"The question is, which bag contains the false coins?"

We leave the fairground behind and continue along the road. After a few minutes of silence, Johanna continues.

She came to the park every day, but she was without a plan. She just knew she had to follow that urge to investigate. The men in black frightened her; she could only walk through the park twice every day, once in the morning and back the other way in the afternoon. Because staring at my window would have given her away, she kept her head pointed straight forward, allowing herself only short sideways glances.

Then, that morning, the goddess of chance appeared in the shape of a dog. Perhaps the goddess was in the squirrel, or perhaps she was in both. Either way, the dog came from the other end of the park, a small, white, fluffy thing, and it chased, yapping and squealing, a squirrel that traversed the grass in quick, jerky bounces, in search of the safety of a nonexistent tree.

Johanna saw her chance. She slipped by the momentarily distracted black coated men, and before she knew it she was standing inside my apartment building, her heart pounding heavily.

When she first saw me in the flesh, after climbing the raggedy steps up to my door, she instantly felt a deep connection to me. I was familiar, like someone from her past, she said, but no matter how hard she tried to pull it out of her mind, she couldn't.

The road continues to snake through the green pastures, towards the ever-elusive tree line. We fall silent again, only our shoes sound out against the dirt with a damp clatter. I want to tell her about everything that happened to me, about the fireplace and Koob, about the Palace and all the stories I've visited, but I can't coax myself across the threshold of beginnings.

I find myself making points in my head. When I'm done I've come up with two. Number one: I want to know about her father. What happened to him? Number two: I want to know what the book was about, the one eerily titled the same as mine. For some reason I feel compelled to ask first about the man behind it.

"Johanna, what happened to your father?"

Our feet march on, the crunching sound the baseline of some strange tune, and I feel from the silence that she is trying hard to formulate an answer that explains it all at once. For the both of us.

"You know, nobody's asked me that before. Not like that. So direct."

I glance behind us – the fairground is now out of sight, and there is only the brown of the road, the green to the sides and the blue above.

"I think it was mostly disappointment." She punctuates the last word with a kind of surprise.

"I don't mean he was struck with anything out of his control, a disease or anything like that, and it wasn't his mind that suddenly turned against him. He chose to go in there. It was a controlled process, and I think he did it out of disappointment."

From out of nowhere, dark clouds have formed, blotting out the blue of the sky, and the colors around us take on a vivid, metallic shine.

"It must have been some disappointment," I say.

She doesn't answer right away.

"It was a choice," she says when she continues. "His mind was so developed – it was a quarterback of a mind with a complete set of skills. It could pass, catch, feint, and tackle, and it could run flat out faster than any other mind around. It saw the limits of life, and it was so disappointed that it turned inside out and crawled into the only place where there were no limits. My father went crazy so as not to go crazy."

With her last words, the rain begins to fall and we start running.

We don't have anywhere to run to, but running seems the only sensible thing to do. After but a minute we spot a tall building emerging through the weather, and when we come close enough I can see the Hotel sign jutting out from its side.

The hotel is a modern cement building rising alone from the flat landscape. Everything about it gives the impression of being perfectly rectangular: the windows cut in the cement, peering lifelessly out across the fields, the entrance door, the hotel sign, the lobby desk, and of course the building itself.

Nobody seems to be around and we huddle in front of a fire that sputters in a rectangular fireplace in the lobby, until we are dry. The rain is still coming down hard, and we pass time wandering back and forth in the lobby, a room the size of a shipping container. Rectangular.

Not a single person passes through – no guests, nor any employees – and it's queer, for the lights are all on, the computer screen behind the counter lit up, and there's the fire. But still we are all alone. I walk past it many times – an opening over which a sign reads *Rooms,* before I lean inside to take a look. It's a stairwell. While waiting for the rain to stop, we begin climbing it to the second floor, through a low but pronounced buzzing that emanates from the fixtures. Our steps echo round the empty space, and I am glad to leave it behind when we reach the second-floor corridor. But as far as worries go, one only changes into another. A man is standing at the very end of the corridor, busying himself, as it seems, with the wall. We walk carefully towards him, but about halfway there he commands us to halt.

"Not another step, please!"

Johanna and I freeze and look at each other, his peculiar ways catching us off guard. But before we can come to a decision to turn around and leave, the man lets out a pearling chuckle, still with his eyes on the wall.

He doesn't face us when he speaks. "This hotel has one hundred rooms. As you can see, I am painting the room numbers by hand."

The "by hand" part he says with a drawn-out *a*.

"I need your help with one thing."

"Sure," I say and look at Johanna.

"Could you do me a favor and tell me how many eights I will have to paint?"

By the time we get back to the lobby the rain has stopped. We leave the hotel and continue along the road towards the forest. Once again the sky is a clear blue, and soon the hotel is out of sight, although the forest is still the same distance away. That's the point when my second question makes itself present again. *The last book in the world.*

She tells me it's gone. It was in a box inside another box that went missing in a move. It hurt her to lose it. That book meant the world to her once, not only for what it contained, the incredible stories, but mostly for where it came from: love. It was the one pure thing left of her father. The summersaults of his mind when it was still well and agile.

When it went missing, a part of her cooled off. It went from a hot orange to a dull grey in no time, and then, when she saw on the news the announcement of the competition that was to be held, what they were calling it, a surviving spark shot from the grayness. She decided to find whoever won, seek up that person and ... well, then hopefully the dots would connect. In the best of cases, she would keep him glowing inside her. At worst, nothing at all would happen. The last ember would flare up once, then die completely. Either way, she wouldn't have lost anything she hadn't already.

I want to tell her about my failed attempts to write the book that means so much to her, but the darts of Amor rain heavily upon me. For as I look at her where she walks by my side, I feel she is the most beautiful woman I have ever seen, and I can't bring myself to disappoint her. So strong is the feeling to protect her innocence that I would rather kill myself than do so.

We walk on in silence. Soon the road again takes us within sight of a building; in fact, there are two buildings, one on each side of the road, and between them a beam is blocking the way.

The houses are exactly the same shape and size, two windowless white boxes, each with a closed door facing the other.

We approach the beam and look around. Nobody's there, and I consider for a minute just crawling under it – it would be easy enough, nothing to stop us – but Johanna must have read my mind, for she nudges my shoulder and walks up to the house on the left.

A number 1 sits in a frame next to the door, and on the other house we discover a number 2.

House number 1 is empty, the walls completely bare except for three light switches in a row, about chest-high. It reminds me of a Greek island, the way the whitewashed walls wrap all around us, the air damp and cool like in a cave.

Next to the light switches sits a small note that states, in very precise handwriting, the rules. We are to figure out which light switch is attached to which lightbulb. The lightbulbs are in house number 2, but we can only enter once.

When we step out from house number 2, the beam is conveniently lifted, and we continue down the road. We walk as if we've always walked together, side by side, our feet and swinging arms keeping a perfect rhythm. The sky is still blue, although there's something in the air – a taste, a vibration – that raises the smallest hairs on the back of my hand. The further we walk, the greater the tension becomes, and in focusing on that tension, I all but miss the world around us and the distant tree line that is suddenly no longer so distant.

Thoughts are pressing my words, the words my tongue, until my mouth feels full of a suffocating yarn. I don't understand why it frightens me, it's childish, but the closer we come to the forest, the more frightened I become. I can sense we are nearing some sort of end.

It's right there, on the other side of the river: there's nothing but the thick dense greenery of the forest, and from where we stand, there's no seeing into it, not even an inch. A bridge runs across the river, a gangly wooden suspension bridge only one man wide. The water is moving rapidly, but it doesn't make much noise. It simply floats by, sloshing forth smoothly without spilling a drop over its edges. Next to it, a few feet from the riverbank, stands a building. It's a square box with a flat roof. *The last bastion*, I think.

If I set foot on the other side I will lose myself, and then there's only the slightest chance that I'll find my way through. I'm sure of it. The thought comes from out of nowhere. But it's the way to go. It's the only way to go, and I already know Johanna won't come with me. Not through there, she won't. I'll be by myself. But before I face any of this I have to know. I've made up my mind. When it's time, no matter what, I have to ask her.

The house holds only one thing: a courtroom. Surprise is by now a stranger, a runaway, lost forever in a cobweb of train tracks, ground to mental dust by endless churning, and a courtroom makes perfect sense. Just as appropriate is the fact that a judge awaits us. And just like the others, he too wastes no time.

"You make a statement."

His voice is boisterous and huge and could probably carry across a large lake or stand out in a bleacher full of screaming fans.

"If it's true, I'll sentence you to four years in prison. If it's false, I'll sentence you to six."

Echoes of the judge's voice still resonate within the courtroom as we step outside. Even though we haven't been gone more than half an hour, a thick darkness has fallen across the land. The river, too, has changed, become audible – perhaps it runs louder in the night – and led by our ears we easily find our way to the edge of the bridge. Before she can say anything, I take the leap.

"So, this is it," I say. I look at the bridge disappearing into the Cimmerian shade, then at Johanna, her face soft and shapeless in the dim light. She reminds me again of what the judge read to us from his stand. It takes seven minutes to get across if I walk. A guard sits on top of the courthouse, and every five minutes he looks at the bridge through the sights of his rifle. Anyone trying to escape to the other side is shot, and anyone trying to get over from the forested side is shot if they don't return immediately.

"Don't forget." Johanna says with the same honey-golden voice she had as a child. "Just do as I say, and you'll get back to where you want to be."

I'm sad, but also proud of the fact that she now has all the answers. Proud that the seeds planted so long ago bore fruit, and sad because I have nothing more to teach her when it comes to riddles.

There's no ceremony. I leave her standing there and move backwards, step by step, until her face is eaten up completely by the darkness. I feel more frightened than ever before. The water gushes below me, spitting and hissing, the cold drops colliding with my face like tiny silver bullets. The planks wobble, and the entire construction sways from side to side. I clench my jaw so hard I feel the pulse beating raw inside each tooth's pulp. But this is the way. I've come a long way, and this is the one way back. This is the way.

I was right. The forest is dense, and so dark I can't see where I'm going. I simply lean forward, and as the brush parts I let myself fall. I pick myself up again and again and start over. Up and down, up and down. I ignore the fear that grasps after me, pulling me back, holding me down. I have no direction. I just go towards the darkest spot inside of me, the place that I have avoided all these years. I aim for it, I close my eyes, and I press forward. Things are tearing and breaking all around me, vines, thorns, barriers, even limbs it feels like, but I don't stop. I won't stop. I refuse to back down.

Everything is black for a while, I could be at the bottom of a lake and not even know it. But somehow I know I'm not at the bottom of anything. For the first time I'm at the other end. I'm surfacing. It's a turning point.

When I regain my senses, I know I've made it through the forest. Light penetrates my closed eyelids; the darkness is gone. I stay where I am for now, savoring the moment. When the time is just right – I sample it like one would a tasty treat – I open them slowly. The fireplace is the first thing I see. It's empty and since long unused. I'm on a mattress; there are bookshelves filled with books all along the walls, a desk stands by my feet, on it a bouquet of flowers, a big bowl of mints, and one of those stress-reliever balls with bulging plastic spikes you can roll under your foot. Below it there's a cart loaded with stacks of books.

I sit up. There are no windows – correction, there are windows, one on each side of the fireplace, but they are both barred and blocked, allowing only a thin slit of light to enter at the very top. Suddenly a door in the wall opens and I turn to face it. Harry. It's Harry.

"You have a visitor, old man."

Harry, redheaded, freckled Harry, I will always remember the picture of him catching that grand fish.

"Sure, Harry, sure, a visitor," I say but am already past the old Harry, well past him, and myself.

All the while, from somewhere above I hear the scratchings. Is it then really so? Have I been so blind to the obvious? At the end of the forest, am I, like all the others, ink and connecting neutrons? A blot of fantasy-seed spilled from the phallic fountain pen? Scratched and carved into a paper...

16

She still moves like a little girl, clutching the book under her arm.

"Thanks, Harry, give my best to Mrs. Hardgrave."

Harry smiles, and her heart flutters like the wings of a spring bird. Not because of Harry, although it's cute the way his freckles part on each side of his mouth as he smiles, but because of Him.

The elevator is old and shaky, and like all aged things it fills her with warmth. The seventh floor, how many times has she not pressed the button and ridden through the old shaft up to the room at the end of the corridor? The hospital library, who would have thought that's where he'd end up?

When the elevator bounces to a stop, her heart settles with the same motion. No matter how often she visits, the lump is always there when she leaves. But today the lump is cracked. A chip has been sledged from it with the impact of a few simple words.

The sun is shining in through iron webs that, even here on the first floor, brace all the windows. As always, Mr. Krista is by the entrance in his black uniform. *Any other place, any other time, it could have passed as a suit,* she thinks while he flashes a great white smile at her, holding open the door.

"How is your father today, Miss Butter?"

At this she shrugs her shoulders and smiles back, a tiny motion, but enough for the book to slip from under her arm. It hits the uppermost step of the stair, the impact bursting its weary and frayed satin seams. A sudden gust of wind blows in across the steps; it grabs the loose papers and sucks them into the air, sweeping them high above the lawn before Johanna or Mr. Krista understands what has happened. Together the two of them scuffle for a second, attempting to catch a few, but they give up almost at once. There's no use. They simply stand there, watching the wind carrying them further and further away.

When they are out of sight, Johanna shrugs her shoulders and starts down the steps.

"Wait! Miss Butter, what about this?"

Mr. Krista bends to pick up the now-empty leather binding. Johanna turns and looks at it, then at Mr. Krista, then at the building, all the way up to the seventh floor, precisely at the two covered windows that flank an old chimney, and just below it the sign that reads Oaktree Asylum, and she begins to laugh. The wind returns and scatters her laughter all across the lawn. Her last words, before she turns to leave, fall like colorful confetti.

"I don't need it anymore."

A few words from the seventh floor against many thousands, and suddenly she doesn't need it anymore. As Johanna steps right across the lawn, Mr. Krista watches her in puzzlement and wonders whether finally the whole family has gone mad. He traces her where she walks, under the old plentiful oaks, tall and majestic trees that reach for the sky, and when she is out of sight he contemplates the piece of leather. It feels so soft against his skin. But then his fingertips reach the outlines; he turns it over. Mr. Krista has to hold it up close to his face to be able to read it. After all these years it's still there, weak but visible, the letters once so carefully stamped by one Jonathan Butter. *The Last Book in the World.*

17

It's raining sideways from a sullen sky. The temperature will drop below freezing tonight. Christmas is around the corner, lots to plan for, and his back hurts from all the sitting, a fist's length above the sit bones. He looks down at the words, the tiny letters in orderly rows, and feels... something. He turns to look around the room, wondering if someone is watching. Not from out there, there's nothing in the window, but from above. Something or someone is watching from above! He exhales, gives it all a rest, and lays down his pen.

JONATHAN'S LIST OF BOOKS
IN ALPHABETICAL ORDER

1. 1984, George Orwell
2. A Clockwork Orange, Anthony Burgess
3. A Farewell to Arms, Ernest Hemingway
4. A Handful of Dust, Evelyn Waugh
5. A House for Mr. Biswas, V.S. Naipaul
6. A Passage to India, E.M. Forster
7. A Portrait of the Artist as a Young Man, James Joyce
8. Absalom, absalom!, William Faulkner
9. All the Kings Men, Robert Penn Warren
10. An American Tragedy, Theodore Dreiser
11. Animal Farm, George Orwell
12. Anna Karenina, Leo Tolstoy
13. Appointment in Samara, John O'Hara
14. Beloved, Toni Morrison
15. Berlin Alexanderplatz, Alfred Döblin
16. Brideshead revisited, Evelyn Waugh
17. Buddenbrooks, Thomas Mann
18. Call it sleep, Henry Roth
19. Catch 22, Joseph Heller
20. Crime and punishment, Fyodor Dostoevsky
21. Dead souls, Nikolai Gogol
22. Death comes for the archbishop, Willa Cather
23. Deliverance, James Dickey
24. Don Quixote, Miguel Cervantes
25. Finnegans wake, James Joyce
26. Go tell it on the mountains, James Baldwin
27. Gone with the wind, Margaret Mitchell
28. Gravity's rainbow, Thomas Pynchon
29. Great Expectations, Charles Dickens
30. Herzog, Saul Bellow

31. Hunger, Knut Hamsun
32. I, Claudius, Robert Graves
33. Invisible Man, Ralph Ellison
34. Light in august, William Faulkner
35. Lolita, Vladimir Nabokov
36. Lord of the flies, William Golding
37. Loving, Henry Green
38. Madame Bovary, Gustave Flaubert
39. Middlemarch, George Eliot
40. Midnight's Children, Salman Rushdie
41. Moby dick, Herman Melville
42. Molloy, Malone Dies, The Unnamable, Samuel Beckett
43. Mrs. Dalloway, Virginia Wolf
44. Naked lunch, William S. Burroughs
45. Native son, Richard Wright
46. Nostromo, Joseph Conrad
47. Old Goriot, Honoré de Balzac
48. On the road, Jack Kerouac
49. One flew over the cuckoo's nest, Ken Kesey
50. One hundred years of soltitude, Gabriel Garcia Marquez
51. Pale fire, Vladimir Nabokov
52. Portnoy's complaint, Philip Roth
53. Pride and Prejudice, Jane Austen
54. Rabbit, run, John Updike
55. Ragtime, E.L Doctorow
56. Revolutionary road, Richard Yates
57. Slaughterhouse-five, Kurt Vonnegut
58. Sons and lovers, D.H. Lawrence
59. The adventure of huck finn, Mark Twain
60. The adventures of augie march, Saul Bellow
61. The age of innocence, Edith Wharton
62. The ambassadors, Henry James
63. The Big Sleep, Raymond Chandler
64. The bridge of san luis rey, Thornton Wilder
65. The brothers Karamazov, Fyodor Dostoyevsky

66. The catcher in the rye, J.D. Salinger
67. The day of the locust, Nathanael West
68. The death of the heart, Elizabeth Bowen
69. The golden notebook, Doris Lessing
70. The good soldier, Ford Madox Ford
71. The grapes of wrath, John Steinbeck
72. The great gatsby, F. Scott Fitzgerald
73. The heart is a lonely hunter, Carson McCullers
74. The heart of the matter, Graham Greene
75. The man without qualities, Robert Musil
76. The moviegoer, Walker Percy
77. The prime of miss jean brodie, Muriel Spark
78. The red and the black, Stendahl
79. The red badge of courage, Stephen Crane
80. The sheltering sky, Paul Bowles
81. The sound and the fury, William Faulkner
82. The stranger, Albert Camus
83. The sun also rises, Ernest Hemingway
84. The tale of genji, Murasaki Shikibu
85. The tin drum, Gunter Grass
86. The trial, Franz Kafka
87. Their eyes were watching god, Zora Neale Hurston
88. Things fall apart, Chinua Achebe
89. To kill a mockingbird, Harper Lee
90. To the lighthouse, Virginia Wolf
91. Tristram shandy, Laurence Stern
92. Tropic of cancer, Henry Miller
93. U.S.A. Trilogy, John Dos Passos
94. Ulysses, James Joyce
95. Under the net, Iris Murdoch
96. Under the volcano, Malcolm Lowry
97. War and peace, Leo Tolstoy
98. Wide sargasso sea, Jean Rhys
99. Women in love, D.H. Lawrence
100. Wuthering heights, Emily Bronte

RIDDLES

THE DWARF

The dwarf spreads his arms and asks us to choose. One way leads to doom and destruction, the other towards salvation. We can ask anything we like, but we only have the one question. And one more thing, only every other time will his answer be truthful.

"What is your question?" The evil dwarf hisses.

Johanna asks her question without hesitating. "Is left the wrong way?"

If left is the wrong way and the dwarf is lying, he will say no, so right will be the way to go.

If left is the wrong way and the dwarf is telling the truth he will say yes, so right will be the way to go.

Right is the answer.

COINS

"You have five bags of coins. Each contains an equal number of coins, but one of the bags contains false coins. False coins weigh eleven units apiece and real coins weigh ten units apiece."

He doesn't look up at us, our eyes never meet; he only watches the bags of coins before him.

"This is a scale. It's only good for one measurement, then it will cease to work."

He looks at the scale and holds it for a brief moment in his hands.

"You may open the bags and touch the coins as you please, but I can assure you there's no way of telling them apart."

Still without a glance at us, he pauses, sharpens his focus, and fires the question we know is coming.

"The question is, which bag contains the false coins?"

With the help of Johanna, Jonathan takes one coin from the first bag, two from the second, three from the third, and so on. If it's the first bag that contains the false coins, everything will weigh 151 units, if it's the second bag that contains the false coins, everything will weigh 152 units, and so on.

EIGHTS

"This hotel has one hundred rooms. As you can see, I am painting the room numbers by hand."

The "by hand" part he says with a drawn-out a.

"I need your help with one thing."

"Sure," I say and look at Johanna.

"Could you do me a favor and tell me how many eights I will have to paint?"

There are twenty eights in total: 8, 18, 28, 38, 48, 58, 68, 78, 89, 98, then 80–88, which adds another ten.

LIGHTBULBS

House number 1 is empty, the walls completely bare except for three light switches in a row, about chest-high. It reminds me of a Greek island, the way the whitewashed walls wrap all around us, the air damp and cool like in a cave.

Next to the light switches sits a small note that states, in very precise handwriting, the rules. We are to figure out which light switch is attached to which lightbulb. The lightbulbs are in house number 2, but we can only enter once.

Johanna and Jonathan turn two of the light switches on, wait a minute, and then turn one of them off. They quickly go to the next house. One light will be on, one off, and one off but still hot.

THE STATEMENT

"You make a statement."

His voice is boisterous and huge and could probably carry across a large lake, or stand out in a bleacher full of screaming fans.

"If it's true, I'll sentence you to four years in prison. If it's false, I'll sentence you to six."

Jonathan: "You'll sentence me to six years in prison."

If it is true, then the judge will have to make it false by sentencing him to four years. If it is false, he will have to give him six years, which would make it true. Rather than contradict his own word, the judge sets Jonathan free.

THE BRIDGE

She reminds me again of what the judge read to us from his stand. It takes seven minutes to get across if I walk. A guard sits on top of the courthouse, and every five minutes he looks at the bridge through the sights of his rifle. Anyone trying to escape to the other side is shot, and anyone trying to get over from the forested side is shot if they don't return immediately.

"Don't forget." Johanna says with the same honey-golden voice she had as a child. "Just do as I say, and you'll get back to where you want to be."

Jonathan walks backwards across the bridge. When the guard spots him, he is ordered back to reality.